Supernova

Social Fictions Series

VOLUME 44

The titles published in this series are listed at *brill.com/soci*

Supernova

By

Patricia Leavy

BRILL

LEIDEN | BOSTON

All chapters in this book have undergone peer review.

The Library of Congress Cataloging-in-Publication Data is available online at
http://catalog.loc.gov

ISSN 2542-8799
ISBN 978-90-04-46748-4 (paperback)
ISBN 978-90-04-46749-1 (hardback)
ISBN 978-90-04-46750-7 (e-book)

This book is printed on acid-free paper and produced in a sustainable manner.

ADVANCE PRAISE FOR
SUPERNOVA

"The trust we build with others after trauma, one cosmic speck after another, can shatter in an instant. We learn this lesson early on in healing, yet negotiating trust as a fraught and imperfect process of becoming proves vital to achieving genuine intimacy. Often, we do not realize this until our sense of security explodes—hence the title of Patricia Leavy's latest installment in the Tess Lee and Jack Miller series, *Supernova*. This might seem like a dark message from the hand of another author, but Leavy lends her characteristic warm light to this painfully relatable tale of trust disbanded and reformed. This fourth novel in the Tess Lee arc offers no fairytale endings, only stories we weave together from the rubble of what once constrained us. But isn't that where the real power lies anyway, in our ability to build trust consciously and intentionally, and to place faith in ourselves throughout that process? We saw in earlier installments of this series how love is very much a verb. This time, Leavy shows us the true meaning of trust, perhaps the ultimate action word. It's a very hopeful thing indeed."
Alexandra "Xan" Nowakowski, Ph.D., MPH, Florida State University

"What do you do when your life explodes? Tess and Jack's relationship is put to the test in *Supernova*. In her latest novel, Leavy addresses themes of trust and communication, and explores whether a betrayal will tear everything apart. I couldn't put this book down until I'd finished the last page. *Supernova* stays with you long after you've finished reading."
Jessica Smartt Gullion, Ph.D., Texas Woman's University

"A powerful journey of love, life, and survival, *Supernova* finds Tess Lee and Jack Miller four years into their romance but face to face with past trauma. Weaving an intricate blend of humor, sadness, and joy,

Supernova will grab you by the heart as you walk with Tess and Jack through the complexities of darkness and light that shape the contours of life."
J. E. Sumerau, Ph.D., The University of Tampa

"Just like its namesake phenomenon, Leavy's fourth Tess Lee and Jack Miller installment, *Supernova*, is a tale that suddenly intensifies in brightness because of a catastrophic explosion that shatters the almost-ordered perfection of the world we have come to know. The central question here is whether love can be real if it is based on dependency. We begin to see how each person who professes to love Tess does not really trust her in the most fundamental way, believing that her past traumas give them the right to protect her from unfolding present ones. The people on the edges of her life are the ones who truly trust her to be whoever she chooses to be, the ones who trust her constantly displayed strength. This is a story about learning to trust those we love, even when we want to shield them from pain, a novel about facing and recovering from trauma, of being a bystander, and accepting the darkest parts of those we love and ourselves. Written for multiple audiences, readers of *Supernova* cannot help but absorb its lessons about the true meaning of trust and the ways in which we must learn to heal so that we can be our best selves for those we love, while being willing to reveal our scars. A perfect choice for book clubs and summer reads, this story becomes an essential part of any college classroom in psychology, history, social work, sociology, or women's studies/gender studies. But it's also a great choice for those teaching criminal justice, forensic science, or intelligence studies. It's a novel you desperately don't want to end, but when it does, you're left once again rewarded and sure that at least Leavy believes the world is filled with better people than we know."
Melissa Anyiwo, Ph.D., Curry College

"Supernovas are space giants whose explosions leave behind both black holes and new stars. This title is the perfect metaphor for the newest chapter of Tess and Jack's saga. *Supernova* tells the story of

the time that comes after the honeymoon, when all the darkness of the past can no longer be ignored or stifled. Both Tess and Jack have to learn that the only way forward is through, through the pain, through the unfinished business, through the guilt and shame with which we torture ourselves, through the forces that can shift one's perception of a relationship in the blink of an eye. This is the cosmic fight between light and darkness, and we see the parallel paths of Tess and Jack's struggle toward the light and the descent into darkness in Tess's parallel universe, her novel called *Morning Sun*. Patricia Leavy has achieved a new level of depth and wisdom, while maintaining the delight of love and friendship on every page. I started reading this book at noon and am writing this blurb before 5:00 p.m. You will want to read it in one sitting, as I did, because it's too good to put down."
Eve Spangler, Ph.D., Boston College

"With a cast of relatable characters and (un)fortunate situations, Leavy gives us another novel about the risks, rifts, and reconciliations we might encounter in our relationships. This is a creative and courageous text that interrogates the residue of abuse and trauma, provides key insights about resilience and advocacy, and offers important lessons about loyalty and self-transformation."
Tony E. Adams, Bradley University

"It has been my pleasure and privilege to read esteemed academic and novelist Patricia Leavy's latest installment of Tess Lee novels. These beautiful and powerful books explore myriad themes including relationships, kind-heartedness, integrity, courage, chosen family, pain, vulnerability, and the power of the arts to heal, challenge, expand, educate, and connect. This latest offering once again demonstrates Leavy's long-standing expertise in arts-based research, together with her talent as an engaging, creative, and important writer. As before, this book gripped me, and I was once more unable to put it down. The texture of Leavy's writing is so inviting, the characters so beautifully and completely drawn that I always feel as if I am in the room with them. A central motif in these books is the love story between Tess (herself a

successful writer) and her Jack (a federal agent). Whilst Tess and Jack appear to have a transcendent love, it is very much grounded in the gritty realities of contemporary life and their own histories, some traumatic. Not to be sugarcoated, Tess and Jack's love story endures sometimes harrowing events. Leavy skillfully creates a world in which we walk with her characters through their dark times as she explores vengeance and violation, but also love, forgiveness, and healing. Indeed, the love stories in this series are multiple, with the core relationship supported by the love of friends, the love of art, and the deep satisfaction and restoration that can be found in creative practice. The themes and the narrative arcs in *Supernova* are important, ethical learning moments. Through pure aesthetic engagement and the experience of the reading, we are privy to the unconditional love of the central characters and the assemblage of their very fine friends. However, this book, like the others, is so much more than a fine example of chick lit. The symbolism is potent and the themes dark. There is deep trauma and its reverberating impacts—survival and healing, social justice, activism and advocacy. Wonderfully and generatively, all of these elements have the arts at their core, in all of the reconciliations and resolutions of the plot. This aspect is as powerful as it is beautiful. I have been honoured to have read all the books thus far in this series, and with each, I glean important experiences and learnings. With *Supernova*, I have taken in the resilience of authentic love, the way vulnerabilities can make us strong, and that we might take control of the only thing we really can: our own decisions. This book is such a strong part of this lovely series. As always, I insist you read them all."
Alexandra Lasczik, Ph.D., Southern Cross University

"After reading the third installment of the Jack Miller and Tess Lee stories, *Constellations*, I found myself talking about Tess and giving advice to my students and colleagues as if each of them knew exactly who Tess Lee is. Tess's journey and her love for humanity had permeated my very soul. Having been given another opportunity to delve even deeper into their lives through the fourth novel in this series, *Supernova*, I could not possibly love this character any more.

This is my favorite version of Tess; I needed this version of Tess Lee Miller. *Supernova* is a book that takes you on a journey of forgiveness, the forgiveness of self and others. Patricia Leavy has a way of guiding you through the dark night of the soul without even leaving your bed. *Supernova* forces the reader to come face to face with biases, triggers, and personal truths in a way that, if you are not paying attention, can shift entire paradigms."
Renita M. Davis, LICSW, PIP, Troy University

"Just when I thought I had found my favorite Tess Lee novel, Leavy's *Supernova* had me glued to the page and the story of Tess and Jack. What do we do when we face the darkness in those we love? What do we do when those we love betray our trust? Tess and Jack show us that love is a muscle that we need to exercise and use if we are to see the light in one another. Don't miss the newest installment in the great love story we all need to read and learn to live."
Sandra L. Faulkner, Ph.D., author of *Poetic Inquiry: Craft, Method and Practice*

"Patricia Leavy is no stranger to the impassioned use of fiction as a way to write about the relational issues that pervade our lives. Her latest novel, *Supernova*, continues this writing streak as she creatively conveys and explores situations of sustained trauma and healing, the impact of violence, and complications related to trust in intimate relationships. What does it mean to trust? How do we go on after others violate our trust? *Supernova* invites readers to think about and feel our own bonds and the trust we do or do not have with others."
Keith Berry, Ph.D., University of South Florida

Selected Fiction from Patricia Leavy

Constellations

Twinkle

Shooting Stars

Candy Floss Collection

Film

Low-Fat Love Stories
By Patricia Leavy and Victoria Scotti

Blue

American Circumstance: Anniversary Edition

Low-Fat Love: Expanded Anniversary Edition

For more information, visit the author's website
www.patricialeavy.com

For everyone, everywhere

CONTENTS

ACKNOWLEDGEMENTS

Thank you to everyone at Brill | Sense for supporting this book and my growth as an author. Special thanks to John Bennett, Jolanda Karada, Els van Egmond, Henriët Graafland, Caroline van Erp, Evelien van der Veer, and Robert van Gameren. Thank you to the editorial advisory board members of the *Social Fictions* series for your generosity, and to the early reviewers for your kind endorsements. Heartfelt thanks to Shalen Lowell, the world's best assistant, spiritual bodyguard, and friend. Sincere appreciation to Celine Boyle, the world's best writing buddy, for the invaluable feedback. Thank you to Clear Voice Editing for the always phenomenal copyediting services. To my social media community and colleagues, thank you boundlessly for your support. My deep gratitude to my friends, especially Tony Adams, Vanessa Alssid, Keith Berry, Renita Davis, Pamela DeSantis, Sandra Faulkner, Ally Field, Robert Charles Gompers, Alexandra Lasczik, Linda Leavy, Laurel Richardson, Xan Nowakowski, Mr. Barry Mark Shuman, Jessica Smartt Gullion, Eve Spangler, and J. E. Sumerau. My love to my parents. Madeline Leavy-Rosen, you are my light and my heart. Mark Robins, you're the best spouse in the world. Thank you for all that words cannot capture. Tess Lee always dedicates her novels to everyone, everywhere. I think she does that because she understands we all need inspiration and a light in the darkness. In the spirit of Tess, this is dedicated to everyone, everywhere.

CHAPTER 1

"Stop, I can't take it," Tess said through bursts of laughter.

"It was so funny. I could hardly breathe," Jack said, snagging the last tortilla chip from the basket. "I can't believe we polished these off."

"We always gorge ourselves here. The mole sauce on those stuffed poblanos was crazy good," she said.

"Hole-in-the-wall neighborhood spots are the best. I know you love this place."

"It's so romantic to be tucked away in the dark corner with you," she said, extending her arm across the table.

He put his hand on hers. "How do you feel about your meeting tomorrow?"

"I'm never going to take the deal," she said, rubbing his hand. "Other than marrying you, the best thing I ever did for myself was deciding to retain the rights to my novels. The last thing I want to do is sell to some huge media conglomerate. They're going to offer a fortune; my team says it'll be a historic deal. They see Tess Lee as a brand."

"Did they pressure you to take the meeting?"

She shook her head. "It's important to me to receive the offer. Writers and other artists go through endless struggles, especially nowadays, when people see us as content creators." She paused and massaged Jack's fingers. "You have no idea what it's like as a woman in my position. I've taken so much abuse. Because I was so young when I started out, they were especially harsh toward me. For years I had to picture myself surrounded in light, like a protective shield, just to power through it. The payoff has been this life I've built, the freedom and creativity, not the wealth I earned. But for the countless others who haven't been as privileged, I need to go and officially hear the offer. I'm doing it for them. Does that make any sense?"

He lifted her hand to his lips and kissed it softly. "Perfect sense. Are you sure you're okay going to New York alone?"

She nodded. "The driver's picking me up after breakfast, I'll jet in for my meeting, and I'll be back in time to meet you all at Shelby's tomorrow night."

"I'm surprised you didn't want Omar to go with you."

"You know how much I love and appreciate him, but this is something I need to do alone. All of this started more than twenty years ago with me and a notebook, just writing. I'm grateful to everyone on my team for all they do to help me, but at the end of the day, the 'Tess Lee empire,' as they call it, well, it's just me. It's my work, my words, my thoughts, my business decisions. For better or worse, I own it."

He smiled and kissed her hand again. "Sweetheart, I'm so proud of you I don't even have the words for it."

"Thank you, baby."

"You know I could've gotten out of this consulting thing if you wanted me to keep you company on the jet."

"Jack, I always want you by my side, but even though you're not working full time for them anymore, I know how loyal you are to the Bureau. Your country needs you. You can't turn away from that. Besides, your dedication is one of the things I love about you. Do you think you'll be able to help?"

"I hope so. If we can't locate any of the members of this terrorist cell, the country is open to all kinds of attacks. Years ago, I was involved in a takedown with some people that could have a connection to these guys. I'm gonna dig through the files and see if I can find something. They've already gone through them with a fine-tooth comb, so it's a long shot, but I might be able to see something they've missed."

"Baby, can I ask you something?"

"Anything," he replied.

"I know how patriotic you are and how you felt called to serve. Knowing your father, I can imagine how those values were instilled in you. But I've always thought there's something else that drives you."

He smiled tenderly, picked her hand up, and caressed her palm. "It's such a special feeling to have someone truly know you."

She smiled.

2

"How can I explain this? When I get on a public bus or a train, I look around at the people: commuters going to work, parents with their kids, people reading books, maybe even a Tess Lee novel. Nothing out of the ordinary, just people living their lives. I look at their faces and in their eyes, and the thought that their lives could be taken from them at any moment, well... Well, I just want to do anything I can to protect them."

"I love you so much," she said, squeezing his hand.

"I love you too, more than I can say."

"Jack, do you ever miss being in the field, out in the thick of it? I didn't know you then, so I don't know what you were like. It's okay, you can tell me if you do."

"No, sweetheart. I gave that up because it wasn't possible to have any kind of personal life." He paused and ran his finger along her hand. "I was good at it. I was really good at doing things that I wish our world didn't need done. After beating the odds and surviving the job, I thought it was time to get a life for myself. I was trying to meet someone, but hadn't stumbled on the right person. Then when I found out about my daughter..." He stopped, took a breath, and wiped his eyes. "When Gracie died, I didn't think my heart would be capable of love again. I thought that I belonged down in the darkness, fighting monsters. I might have gone back after I pulled myself out of that grief, but I met you instead." He lifted her hand to his lips and gently kissed her again. "I've never looked back."

She smiled.

"When we got married, I promised to give you the same level of commitment I had given to my country. That's my priority, which is exactly how I want it to be. I didn't know it was possible to feel this way every day. Tess, *you* are all I want."

She got up, walked to his side of the table, sat on his lap, and draped her arm around him. He ran his fingers through her long hair. They stared into each other's eyes and then kissed passionately.

"I'd better pay the bill," he whispered, caressing the side of her face. "I'm ready to take you home, Mrs. Miller."

CHAPTER 2

Jack, Joe, and Bobby were sitting at their group's regular table at Shelby's Bar halfway through their first round of drinks when Luciana and Gina arrived. Joe stood, kissed Luciana, and pulled out her chair.

"Hey babe," Bobby said to Gina as she sat down.

"Rob was a little fussy before I left. I don't think we should stay long," she said.

"Relax, your mom can handle it. Get a drink," he said, signaling to the waitress. "We could use some time away to chill."

Gina rolled her eyes. "Let's check on them in a little while."

"Sure," he said, grabbing a fistful of pretzels and munching away.

The group ordered drinks and two platters of nachos.

"Where's Tess?" Luciana asked.

"She said she would come straight here when her jet landed. I thought she would have been here by now," Jack said.

"Do you know how her meeting went?" Joe asked.

Jack shook his head. "She texted me when she boarded the jet on her way to New York, but I haven't heard from her since. Ah, there's Omar. He probably knows," he said, taking a swill of his beer.

"Hey hey, everyone. Clay sends his regrets. Life of a surgeon, you know. He had to fill in for someone at the hospital." He raised his arm up to order a beer, then turned to Jack. "Tess isn't here yet?"

"No. Have you heard from her?"

"I texted her this morning to wish her luck, and she responded promptly. Not a word since. Very unlike her. I expected her to run out and call me the moment the meeting was done."

"Hmm," Jack muttered.

"She's being unusually hush-hush. Honestly, I would have thought she'd be here by now. Her meeting ended hours ago. The whole team was on standby waiting to review the official offer, so I called the publisher to have them send it over. They said she left at two and that they were under strict orders from Tess to wait until Monday to send the contract." He picked up a pretzel and continued, "I'm still surprised she didn't want me to go with her. You should have heard the publisher when we were setting this up. They expected her to bring a whole team—assistant, lawyers, the works. They were floored when I said she was coming alone."

"She had her reasons," Jack said.

"I know. We haven't spoken about it, but I understand it's something she needed to do by herself."

"What do you think the terms of the offer will be?" Jack asked.

"We know it will be the biggest offer of its kind in history. It'll be at least two hundred and fifty million for the back catalogue rights. Everyone's guessed somewhere between two hundred and seventy-five and three hundred and fifty million. With how many of those rights she's already licensed out, it's amazing they'll pay so much for what remains."

"That's really remarkable," Joe said. "What she has achieved is mind boggling. Do you think she'll accept the offer?"

"No," Jack said decisively.

"Not a chance," Omar concurred.

Luciana rubbed Joe's arm. "Tess is an artist. It's hard to explain that to someone like…"

"Someone uncreative like me?" Joe asked with a laugh.

Luciana smiled. "It's just hard to explain to someone who isn't an artist. She and I have had many conversations about our work. I understand what her novels mean to her—the words, the characters, the stories. It isn't something you can slap a price tag on, especially not when it means giving up ownership."

The conversation continued. Soon, the group had polished off the nachos and a second round of drinks. Joe and Luciana were dancing and Bobby and Gina were playing darts when Tess finally arrived. She waved hello to her friends and scurried over to the table. Jack's face lit up as he rose to greet her.

"Hey, sweetheart. We were starting to get worried about you," he said, kissing her softly.

"I'm sorry, baby."

"Uh hello, Butterfly, do I get one of those? Well, you know what I mean," Omar said.

She smiled and they hugged.

Jack called to the waitress, "A sparkling water, please, and more nachos."

They all plopped down. Tess turned to Jack and handed him a white paper bag.

"What's this?" he asked.

"I had the driver swing by that bagel place you love on our way to the jet. They had just made a fresh batch of your favorites. Something for the weekend."

"Thank you, sweetheart. You're so thoughtful."

"Kiss me again," she said.

He leaned forward, put his hand on her cheek, and kissed her tenderly.

"I missed you," she whispered.

"I missed you, too," he replied, draping his arm around her.

"Okay, lovebirds, you can finish this at home," Omar joked.

"You don't know what Jack did. It was so romantic."

Omar raised his eyebrows inquisitively.

"When I boarded the jet this morning, it was completely filled with white hydrangeas. There were hundreds of them, and a card that said: "Knock 'em dead, Mrs. Miller. I'm so proud of you. Love, Jack." She looked up at Jack with misty eyes. He caressed the side of her face.

"I love you," he said softly.

"I love you so much," she replied.

Omar smiled. "That's very sweet. Confirms what we all know, that Jack is Husband of the Year every year. You mustn't say things like this in front of Clay. I fear you'll make me look bad. Bringing him a sandwich at work from time to time just doesn't compare to a plane full of flowers."

Tess giggled. "Nonsense. I think that's very romantic, and I'm sure he does too."

"I'm sure he's just happy to be spared from that science experiment his cafeteria tries to pass off as food," Omar replied.

The waitress delivered Tess's drink and the nachos. The others rejoined the table.

"Oh my God, Gina almost poked some guy's eye out with a dart," Bobby said, breaking into hysterics.

Gina playfully hit his arm. "I'm not exactly the best dart player."

"That's an understatement! You could get arrested," Bobby said.

Everyone laughed.

"Well, if you would only dance with me instead, no one would be in imminent danger," Gina quipped.

"Except you. I'd be stomping all over your feet."

Gina rolled her eyes and focused on the group. "Hey, Tess. I'm glad you're here. Maybe you can talk some sense into this one," she said, elbowing Bobby gently in the ribs.

Tess smiled. "Well, I do think you should dance with your wife," she said to Bobby, "but don't drag me into it."

Bobby smirked. "Too late. Someone please save me and change the topic."

Joe smiled and said, "Tess, how was New York?"

"She was just about to tell us," Omar said. "Butterfly, we're dying to hear everything. And where the hell have you been? I know your meeting ended hours ago. We were concerned."

She took a sip of her drink, nuzzled into Jack, and said, "I'm sorry. I needed a little time, so I went to the public library. The librarian recognized me; they were just about to have children's story time, so she asked me if I'd give them a treat and read to the kids. Of course, I said yes."

Omar smiled. "Naturally. Why wouldn't the most famous author in the world randomly stop by a library to read Dr. Seuss to children?"

She threw him the side-eye. "It was Bemelmans' classic *Madeline* books, thank you very much. Anyway, the kids had no idea who I was, which was glorious, but the parents all recognized me and it sort of became a thing. I guess they texted people or posted on social media, because by the time I finished reading a couple of stories, there was a crowd and I had to take pictures with oodles of fans just to get out of there."

Omar laughed. "Bloody hell, Butterfly. You do create drama wherever you go, flitting about and doing your good deeds. Please tell me you at least had personal security with you."

Tess waved him off. "Oh please, you know how I feel about that. I was fine. The driver was outside." She turned to Jack. "Honey, I made a half-million-dollar donation while I was there. I hope you don't mind."

"Don't be silly," he said, kissing her forehead.

"The offer must have been good for you to feel guilt so immediately," Omar said.

She shot him a look. "No guilt, just focusing on what really matters to me."

"Come on, Butterfly, don't keep us in suspense."

"Four hundred and twenty million for the rights and trademarks to the existing works."

"Holy hell, Butterfly. That's absolutely staggering."

"Damn!" Bobby said. "You're a serious badass."

"Congratulations," Joe added.

"Wow!" Jack exclaimed. "I'm so proud of you, sweetheart."

She craned her neck to look up at him and they kissed softly.

"I assume they want new work too, in a separate offer as we insisted," Omar said.

"Yes. That was also sky high, depending on if I committed to three, five, or seven books. An eight-figure signing bonus for each, high royalties, and a cut of merchandising when their studio turns them into movies or shows or whatever, which is to be expected when you join one of the biggest media conglomerates in the world. Of course, I wouldn't own any of the rights to them, and despite their assurances, I would lose creative control."

"Bloody hell. On top of your current net worth, you'd instantly be a billionaire," Omar said. His eyes suddenly welled, and tears started trickling down his face. He wiped them away.

"Sentimental over money, are we?" Tess asked jokingly.

Omar sniffled and shook his head. "Butterfly, I'm proud of you beyond measure. I know what it was like for you to get here. Jack, you can't imagine all the crap thrown her way. Male critics hounded her relentlessly for years in the most sexist, condescending ways. They tried vehemently to inhibit her success, but they never could. Her books are gorgeous. The public loved her. They understood. Not to mention all the industry people who told her she was crazy to run her own publishing, who told her to focus on what she knows, being an artist, and leave the business side to others. And now…" he paused, tearing up again, "and now, on top of everything else you've already achieved, you have this landmark offer for your work."

She smiled. "See, that's one of the beautiful things about old friends: they've seen the journey."

"Butterfly, I remember when you were writing your first novel, *Candy Floss*, between classes in college. God, we were dirt poor. We lived on ramen. I also remember the pressure on you to sign a traditional publishing deal when the book was first making waves. They wanted you to sign away the rights to your next five books. I remember the millions they offered and how desperately you needed money at the time. But you said no. You wanted to own your work, to captain your own ship. And you came up with that industry-changing deal, solely on your own, to retain your rights. It was so brave. I'm still inspired."

She reached across the table. They held hands, smiling at each other, both with tears in their eyes. "I hope you still think it's brave, because once we get the official offer on Monday, I'll be saying no again. I will never sell the rights to my work."

"That's my Tess," Jack said, rubbing her arm.

"Like I said, I'm so bloody proud of you, Butterfly." Omar wiped a tear from his cheek.

"Will everyone be disappointed?" she asked.

"They won't be surprised. We all knew that there was nothing they could offer. Honestly, everyone on the team loves what we're a part of. I don't think they wanted the change, despite the payoff."

Tess smiled. "They'll all be getting seven-figure bonuses from me this year. Perhaps that will soften the blow."

"Your generosity never ceases. Besides, you've made such bloody brilliant moves and investments that you've already amassed more wealth than we could have imagined, and still given hundreds of millions to charity to boot," he said, raising his beer bottle. "Barry's convinced that you'll continue to hit it out of the park, and whatever they offered wouldn't be enough to match the profit you yourself are capable of creating."

"Well that's a change of tune. Usually, he's riding me about my choices and 'over-giving,' as he calls it, which *hello*, isn't a thing."

Omar chuckled. "Yeah, well don't threaten to fire him this week. He is an accountant, Butterfly. He's paid to obsess over the bottom line. I think he's finally accepted that you can continue to donate at the astronomical rate you always have, while still keeping the nest egg quite healthy."

"Oh, so you've all finally accepted that I actually know what I'm doing? About time. It only took you twenty years and nearly a billion dollars."

"Don't get too excited. Personally, I still think you've just gotten lucky," Omar said.

She picked up a pretzel and flung it at him, and they both dissolved into a fit of laughter.

"Honestly, Butterfly, bloody well done."

She tilted her chin in recognition.

"Claire will be relieved; she's been a nervous wreck. You are her golden goose. She's been terrified that you'll start laying your eggs elsewhere," Omar said.

"Oh, please. I told her I had no intention of changing publishers. She's flying in for the Libraries and Literacy Black and White Gala next weekend. I'll reassure her in person."

"Speaking of which, I can't believe you agreed to go. I know how you feel about those events," Omar said.

"Yeah, well, Jack and I are making an exception. It's always been one of the causes nearest and dearest to me. I want to do my part. Besides, Jack looks so handsome in a tux. I can't resist the opportunity."

Jack kissed the top of her head.

"Tess, I'm curious—if you knew you weren't interested, why'd you take the meeting in New York?" Bobby asked.

"I've learned that it's always important to listen to people. Beyond that, this was to be the biggest offer of its kind, and I felt it was important to let them put it on the table. I needed to receive the offer. I never thought it was about me; this was for authors and artists. And for women."

"Absolutely," Luciana said, raising her wine glass.

"I knew you'd understand," Tess said as they toasted.

"Butterfly, at the risk of you throwing that basket at me, you should know there's a ton of media interest in this deal. From *Newsweek* to *Vogue*, everyone wants to land an interview with you. You know what the lead time is like with magazines, but they're all offering to bump their forthcoming issues to fast-track this. You could have any cover you want; even the fashion mags are willing to forgo the normal models and actresses. Bonus for being ridiculously beautiful on top of brilliant."

She lobbed a pretzel at him.

"So, is that a no?" he asked, dodging the pretzel.

"Actually, I'll do it."

Omar's eyes were like saucers. "I... I'm stunned. We all know how you hate PR."

"I have some things to say about artists and about women in business. It's why I went. But I don't want to be interviewed; I'll write an essay. Why don't you get back to them and see who will let me do it on my terms. Tess Lee, in her own words."

"They'll all say yes. You'd be the catch of the year, especially since you haven't done TV or magazines for eons."

"Then let's go with *Vogue*. I want this to reach women. Please find out how many words they want. I know they'll demand a fashion spread, but if I must, there must also be books, pens, notebooks, or computers in every picture. We're promoting reading and women in business. Let's keep it literary."

"Good call. I'm on it," Omar replied.

Jack rubbed Tess's arm and whispered, "I'm so proud of you."

She turned to look at him. "Thank you, baby." She refocused on the group. "Enough about me. What were you all up to today?"

"Well, your guy really helped us out," Bobby said. "We're a lot closer to eliminating a major threat because of him."

"That's great," she said, looking up at Jack.

"It was nothing. Just helped out a little," Jack said.

"Ah dude, it was more than a little. Jack scoured his old undercover files, got in touch with a former contact, and ultimately, he led us to a member of this terrorist cell we've been hunting for months to no avail. A team pulled him in a few hours ago, and he's being interrogated as we speak."

"Jack was brilliant," Joe added. "Truly."

"Baby, I'm so proud of you," Tess said.

Jack smiled. "How about I take you for a spin on the dance floor and we can celebrate this eventful day?"

"I'd love that," she replied. She turned to the group and said, "Come on, who's dancing?"

"Bobby and I should get home. The baby was fussy today and I don't want to leave my mom for too long. Besides, he'll never dance with me anyway," Gina said.

Bobby rolled his eyes. "Okay guys, we're outta here. Tess, congrats again."

"Luciana and I will join you," Joe said.

Luciana smiled.

"Don't worry, Omar, you can have the next dance," Tess said.

"How long have you known me, Butterfly? You know I don't dance in American bars."

"There's a first time for everything," she replied with a shrug.

"I'd have to be bloody drunk, and I'm not there yet," he jested.

"Drink up. Jack and I will be back."

Jack stood, took Tess's hand, and led her onto the dance floor. He pulled her close and they started to sway. "I thought about you all day, sweetheart. I was glad to have an urgent project to focus on. How did it feel to attend the meeting on your own?"

"Really good. They had a huge boardroom set up with at least a dozen bigwigs, and just me at one end of the table, listening, my life's work laid out before me."

"I know I keep saying it, but I'm so proud of you, sweetheart. I really am."

"That means a lot to me," she said, melting into his chest. "I'm proud of you too. I know you prefer to be modest, but you're a hero, Jack."

He blushed.

"You are," she said, pulling back to look in his eyes. "I love you so much."

"I love you with my whole heart, forever. I hope Omar doesn't decide to dance because I can't wait to get you home so we can have a private celebration."

She giggled. "I'm all yours."

***

"Hey, sweetheart, the coffee is ready," Jack said, handing Tess a mug the next morning.

"Thank you, baby."

"That was a monster run. I'm starving. Let's bust into the bagels. I know you never indulge, but these are the best," he said, holding the bag up. "Want one?"

"I'll start with a half."

He smiled. "Grab the juice. Let's eat in the living room."

She pecked his cheek and poured two glasses of orange juice.

They settled onto the couch and bit into their bagels.

"Oh my God, these are so good," Jack said. "Sweetheart, yesterday after your meeting, you didn't call me or Omar. You went to the library instead, and…"

"I'm sorry, honey, it's…"

"There's nothing to be sorry for. That's not what I mean. It's just that I always thought you've done so much to support libraries because you love books and reading, but last night I realized there's more to it. I didn't want to say anything in front of everyone. I was going to mention it when we got home, but then we…"

"Couldn't keep our hands off each other," she said with a giggle.

"Yeah."

She glanced down and softly said, "You know me so well."

He put his bagel down and reached for her hand. "Do you want to tell me?"

"When I was growing up, my grandfather and my uncle would…"

He rubbed her fingers as she steadied her breathing.

She looked into his soft blue eyes and continued. "Well, they would usually assault me after school when my dad was at work. My mom was oblivious. Or they would do it on the weekends if my parents went out during the day. So I made plans to go to friends' houses and do after-school activities as much as I could, but those things didn't happen every day. There was a library not far from our house. When I turned thirteen, I convinced my mother to let me ride my bike there. I went there after school nearly every day and on weekends too. The days I went to the library, I could usually avoid being raped."

"Oh sweetheart, come here," he said, moving close and enveloping her in his arms. "I love you. You're safe now," he whispered.

When they eventually parted, Tess said, "Do you know where a person of any age can go year-round, somewhere inside and safe, where no one asks you any questions and it doesn't cost anything? Public libraries. That's it. Libraries aren't just about books and reading. They're a safe space for all kinds of people, for all kinds of reasons. On top of that, they house imagination and knowledge, and people desperately need those things too. As soon as I became successful, I vowed to do everything I could to give back to libraries. It's why I've donated and raised so much money, and why I spent so many years giving talks and doing book tours even though it was grueling."

"Does Omar know?"

She shook her head. "I never saw any reason to talk about it."

"Thank you for trusting me with it."

She smiled. "Remember the other night when you told me how you see people on a bus and think about how they could become victims of terrorism? How you want to do anything you can to protect them?"

"Yes."

"That's how I feel when I walk into a library. I look around and wonder who is using it as a safe, warm place to escape. I want to do everything I can to help them and to make sure they always at least have that place, and that it's as nice as it can be."

He leaned forward and kissed her lightly. "Just when I think it's impossible to love you more, you reveal something that makes my heart grow."

She gently ran her fingers along his temple and whispered, "We're so connected. We understand each other."

"I know, baby. And now I understand why you agreed to go to the gala next week. I know how uncomfortable you usually feel at those things, the way everyone clamors for your attention."

"Well, the cause is important, but I have to confess that I do have an ulterior motive," she said with a mischievous look.

"Oh yeah, what's that?" he asked, a smile spreading across his face.

She leaned forward and put her hand on the back of his head. "You look so damn sexy in a tux. I'm distracted just thinking about it now."

They kissed passionately, Jack running his fingers through her hair.

"The bagels can wait," she said. "Let's work up an appetite."

He grabbed her and they toppled onto the couch.

CHAPTER 3

Jack stood in their bedroom, straightening his tuxedo tie. Tess emerged from the bathroom in a strapless, white, tulle gown with a full skirt speckled in crystals, her gold heart locket dangling from her neck, her long hair in loose spiral curls, her lips stained pink. Jack's jaw dropped. He put his hand over his heart. "I'm speechless."

She smiled. "All the women usually wear straight, black gowns at these black and white events. So I thought…"

"You'd be the light in a sea of darkness."

She blushed. "You are so handsome. Honey, will you finish zipping me up?" she asked, turning her back to him and holding the bodice of her gown against her chest.

He came up behind her, put his hands on her waist, and blew softly on the nape of her neck. She quivered. He began to unzip her gown. She spun to face him and said, "That's not what you're supposed to be doing."

"Make love with me, Tess."

"Baby, the car is waiting."

"Let it wait."

"But my hair and makeup are done. I can't get all messed up. There's no time to fix it."

He gently ran his fingers along her hairline, leaned forward, and just barely pressed his lips to hers. "I won't kiss you again. Your hair will be untouched. I promise you will be perfect. Trust me," he whispered.

She smiled coyly and let her gown fall to the floor. He took his pants off, picked her up, and she flung her legs around his waist. Holding her, he walked over to an ottoman and sat down with her on top of him. He brushed the side of her face gently and whispered, "You are so beautiful." They made love, their eyes glued to each other, their faces so close they could feel the other's breath, but their lips never touched. After, they sat trembling, holding each other and trying to catch their breath. They touched their foreheads together and closed their eyes.

"I'm so in love with you," Tess whispered.

"I'm so in love with you," Jack whispered back.

Tess pulled back to look at him. "I've never wanted to kiss someone more than I want to kiss you now."

He lightly cupped her face in his hands and just barely grazed his lips with hers. They smiled. "See? I promised you'd still be perfect. And when we get home later, we're going to lie in bed and kiss for hours."

"Now I have something to look forward to," she said, tracing his jawline with her fingers. "We had better get dressed. We're so late."

Fifteen minutes later, they were in the car on their way to the gala. Jack put his arm around Tess and she leaned against him.

"Baby, why didn't you want to wait until we got home?" she asked.

"You were just so damn pretty."

"Oh really?" she asked, looking up at him.

"The spotlight is always on you at these events and I know how that makes you feel," he said, running a fingertip along the side of her face. "I wanted you to be able to picture the look in my eyes and I wanted to remember the look in yours. Nothing else matters. Only how we see each other."

"I can't wait to get home to kiss you," she said, smiling.

Before he could respond, Tess's cell phone rang. She opened her crystal-adorned clutch and retrieved her phone. "It's Omar, probably wondering where we are," she said, swiping to answer the call.

"Hi, Omar. You're on speaker. We're on our way. We got held up," she said with a wink.

"Butterfly, I just wanted to prepare you. It's a Who's Who of people you know."

"Oh really? Who's there?"

"Well, as you know, Claire flew in from LA. Let me tell you, she's feeling a bit possessive over you. She's terrified that you're going to take that astronomical deal and jump ship to join the evil empire. Normally she strokes your ego, but Butterfly, tonight you'll be boosting hers."

Tess giggled. "I don't know what she's so worried about; I told her I would never sell my rights. Who else is there?"

"There's a potpourri of those oil barons you can't stand. Bernard, Dick, the whole lot of them."

"Well, that's good news. As insufferable as they are, no one has deeper pockets than billionaires and we *are* trying to raise money, after all. I plan to personally convince them to give generously."

"Always thinking of the cause," Omar said.

"That's the whole point."

"Butterfly, that's not all. There's someone here you definitely won't be happy to see, the master misogynist reviewer himself, Max Andrews."

"I couldn't care less."

"That's big of you. Always taking the high road."

"I wouldn't go that far. Just tell me this, are you seated with us?" she asked.

"Yes," he replied. "Clay and I are waiting with bells on, or penguin suits that is. And we look dashing, if I do say so myself."

Tess laughed. "Fantastic. We'll have a fabulous time."

"Butterfly, one more thing. There's someone else here who you're not expecting to see."

"Who?"

"Raj is here."

"Raj?"

"He's here on his own. Already approached me. I didn't want you to be caught off guard. I know it's been ages. He's eager to see you."

"It will be nice to see him too. Listen, I'm going to hang up. We're almost there. Bye."

Jack took her hand. "I can't believe Dick Clayton is there. That guy's really an asshole."

"I know, baby, but I care about this cause and his company donates a lot. Making small talk for an evening is hardly that big a price to pay."

"I don't like the way he talks about women, especially you. When he looks at you, it's like he's running some kind of porno flick in his head. It pisses me off."

"He's a jerk, but sometimes at these things we just have to smile and play nice. Please, you can do that, right?"

"Yes, sweetheart." He picked up her hand and gently kissed it. "I know what this means to you. I'll be civil. I just hope he doesn't antagonize me."

"Just remember, baby: it's me and you, nothing else matters."

He kissed her hand again and asked, "Who's Max Andrews?"

"The critic who branded me the people's high priestess of pain."

"There's another asshole I'd like to give a piece of my mind."

"Baby, it's fine," she said, rubbing his arm. "I don't give him a single thought and neither should you."

"What about Raj?"

"Someone I dated a long time ago. Haven't seen him in nearly ten years. He's a lovely man. You'll like him."

"I know I promised not to mess you up, but just one kiss," he said. He put his hand on her chin and pulled her toward him, lightly pressing his lips to hers. "Tess, I love you. I can't wait to watch you sparkle, like you always do, and then I can't wait to get you home so we can be alone."

She smiled, stroking the side of his face.

Just then, the driver pulled up in front of the venue, announcing, "We're here."

"Thank you," Jack said. "I'll get the doors. Tonight, my wife is all mine."

CHAPTER 4

"The entire place looks as if it were designed by Coco Chanel. It has such an elegant feel," Tess remarked to Jack as they strolled arm in arm into the art deco ballroom. Waiters passed around flutes of champagne, sparkling water, and Kir Royale, the only pop of pink in the room, glowing under dimly lit chandeliers. A swing band played lively tunes and couples sashayed across the dance floor. As Tess predicted, the room was littered with women in sleek, black evening gowns, necks dripping with diamonds. Everyone turned to look at Tess when she entered, a ray of light amidst the darkness. Acquaintances immediately hurried to greet them. Oil tycoons Dick Clayton, Bernard Bentley, and several others were huddled together by the bar. They all turned and gestured at Tess, and Dick gave her a smarmy wink. She nodded politely in acknowledgment. Omar and Clay came rushing over.

"Tess, you look absolutely stunning. I don't know whether to call you Butterfly or Firefly, the way you're lighting up the night," Omar said.

"Yes, you look beautiful as always. Like a princess," Clay said, pecking her cheek.

"Thank you both. As promised, you are dashing as ever," Tess replied. "So, tell me…" but before she could finish her sentence, Claire flitted over.

"Tess, what a gorgeous gown," she said, hugging her. "Hi Jack, lovely to see you."

Jack smiled and said, "Hello, Claire."

"You look wonderful as always," Tess said.

"Oh please, I'm wearing the tightest Spanx in the world and I'm afraid you can still see my tummy," Claire said, smoothing the front of her long, black, silk gown. "I just want you to know that we're all set for the auction later. Your book will be the final item of the night. I made sure they know how to treat you. The bidding will start at twenty-five hundred dollars, but they're hoping to get more than ten times that."

Tess smiled.

Without taking a beat, Claire continued, "Oh, and I told the team you weren't happy with that cover option. They'll have new mock-ups for you early next week. I promise you that…"

"Claire, take a breath. We don't need to work tonight. Let's just focus on the charity. It seems you need a glass of bubbly," Tess said, raising her hand to signal for a waiter.

"Tess, I've heard all the rumors. Well, they're not rumors. Now that the two biggest houses have merged, they've formed the most powerful entity in the publishing world. They believe they can have any author they want, and they want you."

"Claire, I told you I'm not interested," Tess said patiently.

"I heard they offered over four hundred million to buy all the rights and trademarks you hold. It would be the biggest deal of its kind, historic. I could hardly blame you for mulling it over. My God, you'd be a billionaire! But if they bought your back catalogue, of course they'd want your future work and I just hope you're as happy working with me as I am…"

Tess put her hand on Claire's arm to slow her down. "Look at me. I turned them down flat. I will never sell my rights. There's no price, no number. We've worked together for twenty years, and I've always been straight with you. Besides, you know what I care about, owning my art. Even if it were worthless to the rest of the world, it would be invaluable to me. So, ignore the whispers and have a splendid time tonight."

Claire smiled. "I'm sorry. You know how I get. Plus, I took half a Xanax on the plane last night with a glass of wine and I think that was a no-no. Between that and the jetlag, I'm a bit out of sorts."

Tess giggled. "Perhaps you can find an attractive man to take you for a spin around the dance floor and work off some of that nervous energy. That man over there has been staring at you," she said, tilting her chin.

Claire craned her neck to look and the man strutted over. "Excuse me, would you like to dance?" he asked.

Claire turned back to the group, said, "I'll see you all at our table later," and walked off with the handsome stranger.

"Nice one, Butterfly. You managed to get Claire off your back and matchmake, all at once," Omar said, raising his glass.

"Two birds, one stone," Tess jested.

Jack turned to her and said, "Sweetheart, would you like to…" but was interrupted when Raj walked over.

"Raj, it's wonderful to see you," Tess said, leaning in to hug him.

He returned her embrace, kissing her cheek. "You look breathtaking."

She smiled. "This is my husband, Jack. Jack, this is my old friend Raj."

"Pleased to meet you," Jack said, extending his hand.

"Likewise," Raj said. "You are a lucky man. How long have you two been married?"

"Four years," Tess replied, intertwining her arm with Jack's. "Did you ever marry?"

Raj nodded. "Some things aren't meant to last."

"I'm sorry to hear that," Tess replied.

"I've kept up with your career. I've read all of your novels; the last one was marvelous, especially the metaphors. And of course I've seen the television shows and movies, although I imagine you still don't watch any of them yourself."

Tess laughed. "No, I don't. What about you? Your company is certainly doing well. You've become the gold standard. Schools and librarians have endorsed you across the board."

"It wouldn't have happened without you," he replied.

"Nonsense. It was all you." Tess turned to Jack and said, "Raj developed an incredible online literacy program."

Raj blushed. "And what do you do, Jack?"

"I was an agent with the FBI for most of my career, specializing in counterterrorism. Now I do consulting for various agencies, national security stuff mostly, and I volunteer with an organization that supports veterans."

"Wow, I'm impressed. I always wondered who would land you, Tess. I knew it would be someone doing good in the world."

"Yes, I'm very lucky," she said, rubbing Jack's arm. "Sometimes we meet the right person at the right time."

"Uh, speaking of the wrong person, incoming," Omar said, as Max Andrews approached.

"Tess Lee, after all these years," Max said.

"Hello, Max."

"You still look gorgeous," he said.

"And you look… older," she replied.

"Please tell me you don't still hate me. The way I look at it, I did you a favor. I made you a star."

Tess huffed. "Really, is that how you see it?"

"Is there any other way?" Max asked with a little laugh.

Omar smiled and looked down.

"I'm always amazed when a man takes credit for a woman's career, to which he's contributed nothing," Tess said. "Perhaps you've forgotten, but when you wrote your little review of my third novel, I already had two award-winning international bestsellers and had negotiated what is still considered to be a landmark publishing deal. But I'm being rude. Allow me to introduce you to everyone." She put her hand on Jack's bicep and said, "Max, this is my husband, Jack. He's devoted his life to fighting terrorism, and in the process, he's saved countless innocent lives. And you may remember my friend, Omar. He's helped inspirational novels reach millions of readers, and he's contributed to arts and peace research that has had a global impact. His husband, Clay, is a trauma surgeon and, like Jack, has also saved countless lives. Finally, this is my old friend Raj. His innovative literacy program has helped millions around the world. Of course you know what I've done with my life, creating a body of literature that will be here long after I'm gone. Remind me, how exactly have you used *your* life?"

Max stood silently for a moment, his mouth agape, as everyone else tried to conceal the smiles flashing across their faces.

Tess smiled before continuing. "I'm not surprised you've tried to glom onto my legacy. After all, what's yours? So, to answer your question, no, I've never hated you. I only ever felt sorry for you. Be well and enjoy your evening."

"Enjoy your evening, Tess," Max said contritely before slithering away.

As soon as he was gone, everyone cracked up.

"Holy hell, Butterfly, that was epic. You are brilliant," Omar said.

"Well done," Clay added.

Jack kissed her cheek and whispered, "Damn, remind me to stay on your good side."

Tess giggled.

"Tess, I can see you haven't changed a bit. Would you like to dance? We have so much to catch up on," Raj said.

She turned to Jack and handed him her purse. "Honey, do you mind?"

"Of course not," he said, pecking her cheek.

Raj took Tess's hand and led her to the dance floor.

"Jack, I have to give you a lot of credit. If Clay's exes and admirers were always popping up all over the place, I don't think I'd cope with it as well as you do," Omar said.

"I know what Tess and I have. What's the deal with this Raj guy, anyway? He seems nice enough."

"They dated for a few months, which was an epically long relationship for her. Before you, he was the only person I ever thought she might settle down with. Of course she never loved him like she loves you, never really loved anyone until you." Omar paused, glanced at the dance floor, and then continued, "I always thought Raj was a stand-up guy, although I had the distinct impression that the feeling wasn't mutual. We never got on as well as I'd hoped. He was a literacy specialist at a public high school when they met, earning a pittance, but he had an idea for literacy software. Tess helped him develop a business plan and hooked him up with venture capitalists. They broke up long before he got going, but today the software is worth millions. Like Tess, he wasn't driven by money. He was driven by a purpose; I suspect he still is. Tess is so good-natured that she personally endorsed his program on many occasions, even though he was no longer in her life."

"Why'd she break up with him?" Jack asked.

"She didn't. He's the only person who ever broke up with her. She didn't say why, just that it was over. I know his family wanted him to marry someone Indian. Perhaps that was the reason."

Jack turned his attention back to Tess, watching Raj lean in close and whisper to her as they spun around the dance floor. When the song ended, they began to meander back to the group but were intercepted by Dick Clayton. He took Tess's hand and led her back to the dance floor. Raj returned alone.

"I see Dick Clayton got his paws on Tess," Omar grumbled.

"That guy's an ass," Jack said, his eyes fixed on Tess. "Maybe I should go cut in."

"Raj, how could you let that buffoon trap her?" Omar asked.

Raj snorted. "He asked her if she'd like to dance and she said yes. He hardly clubbed her over the head and dragged her across the room. But I see some things never change."

"What does that mean?" Omar asked.

"You were always wildly overprotective of Tess. She's not a child. In fact, she's the most accomplished woman in this or any other room. My goodness, did you hear how she handled Max Andrews? Perhaps she deserves more respect."

"Touché," Clay said.

Omar turned and stared daggers at him.

Clay continued. "I'm sorry, Omar, but I've thought it for years. Tess is a grown, highly capable adult. You treat her like…"

"Like what?" Omar asked angrily.

"Look, I know you mean well and that it comes from a place of love, but sometimes you and Jack can both be a bit overbearing. My God, she's simply dancing with someone at a gala, someone you told me earlier she wants to secure a donation from, and the two of you are watching as if he's about to murder her," Clay said.

"She did tell me she wanted to persuade him to support the cause. You know she cares more about the charity than her own personal comfort," Jack said.

Raj looked at Jack and said, "Despite my fear of overstepping, I can't help but say perhaps you and Omar should respect her wishes. If the charity is more important to her, let her make that decision and leave her be. She's already made it clear tonight that she can more than handle things herself."

Clay tried to conceal his smile. Jack ignored Raj and redirected his gaze to Tess.

Omar became increasingly agitated. "You know, Raj, I'm curious: if you understand what's best for Tess, why on earth did you end your relationship? Seems you harbor feelings for her even now."

"Did Tess say that I broke up with her?"

"Didn't you?" Omar asked.

Raj laughed. "She really is a class act. What I did was incredibly stupid, but I wasn't so foolish as to end our relationship. She ended things, although I suppose I didn't leave her much choice."

Omar raised an eyebrow.

"I gave her an ultimatum that she couldn't comply with, so she ended it."

"What kind of ultimatum?"

"It was about you, actually. I wasn't comfortable with your relationship. I felt you were too involved in her life, and I demanded she distance herself from you." He huffed. "I always regretted pushing her away, but now I see that you still treat her like a porcelain doll, all these years later."

"That's wildly unfair. There are reasons why Tess and I look out for each other, and there are certainly reasons why her husband watches out for her. I'm surprised you'd pass such harsh judgment," Omar said.

"You're right. It isn't my place. But I can tell you this—just spending a few minutes with her tonight, I remember how massively impressive she is. The men she spends the most time with should see that too and realize she's perfectly capable of looking out for herself. I've clearly offended you, so I'll leave you now. Enjoy your evening, gentlemen," he said.

As soon as Raj was out of earshot, Omar turned to Clay. "I can't believe you."

"Honey, please don't blow this up into a thing. I was merely saying that, as a long-time observer of your relationship with Tess, he had a point. I'm sorry, but I do think you and Jack can be overprotective."

27

"Raj has no idea about Tess's childhood, her family, or any of the things she's survived. She never told him anything. Nor does he understand the enormous pressure she's under, living in the spotlight and bombarded by fans sharing their sob stories. So he doesn't understand, he couldn't possibly. But you, you should know better. Loving someone isn't a bad thing."

"Omar..."

Omar put his hand up, announced, "I'm going to the bar," and stormed off.

Clay looked at Jack. "I'm sorry. I hope I didn't offend you, too. Tess is your wife. I have no place to say anything."

"It's fine. I realize that I'm a little overprotective sometimes; it's just that I love her so much and I want to take care of her. But I do respect her completely, and Omar does too."

Tess sauntered over, beaming. She intertwined her arm with Jack's. "So, I just got Dick to pledge a hundred-thousand-dollar donation. Bernard and the others will match it. That's over half a million dollars and we just got here!"

"That's wonderful, sweetheart," Jack replied.

"Where are Omar and Raj?" she asked.

Clay looked at his feet.

"Oh dear, did they go at it?" she asked.

"A little bit," Jack said. "Omar said that he always liked Raj, but it wasn't mutual. Let's just say, that became clear very quickly."

Tess grimaced. "Well, I'm sure it makes me a terrible friend, but I think I'll leave them to lick their own wounds because I've been hoping to dance with you all night, my love."

Jack smiled. "There's nothing I'd like more."

"Excuse us," Tess said to Clay as she and Jack walked arm in arm to the dance floor. He placed his hand on the small of her back, pulled her close, and said, "You are the most spectacular woman in the room. Dance with me all night."

"I'm all yours."

They danced for ages, Jack refusing to allow anyone to cut in, until it was time to join their table for the first course. Claire talked

Tess's ear off about various publishing matters and the others made small talk. Before long, they had finished their entrees.

After the waiter cleared their plates, Omar excused himself to go back to the bar.

"Don't you think you've had enough?" Clay asked.

"No, I do not," he replied, stomping off.

"He's just not going to let this go," Clay said, shaking his head.

"What exactly happened?" Tess asked.

"Sweetheart, it's probably best to leave it alone," Jack said. "The auction will be starting soon. How about another whirl around the dance floor before the bidding begins?"

"I'd love to."

Omar stood at the bar, nursing a drink and watching Tess and Jack from a distance. Raj approached him.

"Listen, Omar, I'd like to apologize for my rudeness earlier. It wasn't my place to say anything. I hope you'll apologize to Jack for me as well."

"It's fine," Omar said, taking a gulp of his drink.

"I can see it's not," Raj said.

"You basically said my relationship with Tess is unhealthy. You may not understand this, but Tess is my family. We are family. It's why we look out for each other."

"Then you're lucky to have each other. Again, my apologies. I truly didn't mean to offend. It's not easy to see Tess here tonight, so happy with another man. She's an extraordinary woman. The person I'm really angry with is myself. Anyway, it was good to see you again."

Omar was about to say something, but as Raj walked away, Dick Clayton sidled over. "Well, hello there, Omar," he said, in his thick southern drawl. He turned to the bartender. "Bourbon," he commanded. The bartender handed him a glass and Dick said, "Well hell, cheers, Omar."

"Cheers," Omar said, and they clinked glasses.

"That Tess, she's really something," Dick said, gesturing to the dance floor. "Squeezed me out of a cool hundred grand. Course, she could get a lot more out of me if she wanted, if you know what I mean. Between us, I was hoping she would have ditched that husband of hers by now."

"Well, I hate to disappoint, but I don't see that happening. Jack is the love of her life," Omar replied coolly.

"I don't know what she sees in a thug like that. He ain't worth shit. A real man builds his fortune."

"Like you inherited yours from your daddy?" Omar muttered.

"What's that?"

"Nothing. "It's just that some would call Jack an American hero."

"Ain't no such thing. Others would call him an opportunist. I suppose that's why he married her. Not that she ain't a great little package. But he'll probably walk off with half her fortune one of these days when she's past her prime," Dick said, taking a swill of his drink.

"Wrong again. If it ends, he won't get a cent," Omar said. Instantly realizing what he'd let slip, his entire body clenched.

"Ha! Well, I'll be damned. Tess is such a bleeding heart; never thought she'd make a man sign a prenup. Good for her. Guess she developed a thick skin after all." He gulped the rest of his drink and said, "See ya later," moseying off.

Omar made a beeline to Tess and Jack.

"Do you want to cut in?" Tess asked.

"Uh, actually I need to speak with Jack for a minute. I think they're getting ready to start the auction, so you should probably take a seat."

Tess leaned forward and kissed Jack. "I'll see you at the table, baby."

"Jack, let's find a place to speak privately," Omar said, directing him to a quiet spot by the wall.

"What's up?" Jack asked.

"I did something stupid. I let it slip to Dick Clayton that you signed a prenup before marrying Tess."

"Omar, why would you do that? Tess doesn't know about it. If she ever finds out…"

"I know, I know. I'm so sorry. It just happened. I was upset about what Raj said, had too much to drink, and Dick came over. You know what he's like. If you had heard the things he was saying. It just slipped out. But honestly, I can't imagine why he'd say anything to Tess. I mean, for starters, I'm sure he thinks she knows about it, as would normally be the case, so why would he mention it?"

"I can't take that chance. I have to tell her."

"She'll be furious with me," Omar said.

Just then, the host took to the stage to begin the auction.

"Damn it. I'll tell her after," Jack said. "Come on, let's go back to the table."

The auction proceeded with rare bottles of wine selling for fifteen thousand and several signed books and scripts going for up to forty thousand. The auctioneer finally introduced the last item of the evening: a signed, first-edition copy of *Candy Floss* from Tess Lee's personal collection. The bidding began at two thousand and five hundred dollars and was quickly up to forty thousand. From two tables over, Raj held up his paddle and bid fifty thousand dollars. Tess glanced over and mouthed, "Thank you." He smiled in return. He was soon outbid as Bernard Bentley and Dick Clayton went back and forth, trying to outdo each other. With a final price of two hundred and fifty thousand dollars, Dick was declared the victor.

"Holy hell, Butterfly. Well done," Omar said, raising his glass.

"That's an astonishing price. You have some real fans," Claire said. "But of course, you're worth it."

"Yes, Dick's a brute, but he's loose with the company's purse strings if only to make himself look like a nicer person than he is," Tess replied.

Jack laughed, leaned over and kissed her cheek. "Well done, baby."

"I really should go over and thank him," she replied, standing up.

Jack watched as she walked over.

"Why didn't you stop her?" Omar asked.

"What was I supposed to do?" Jack said, nervousness in his voice.

He watched as Tess hugged Dick. They chatted for a few minutes, but then Tess suddenly looked directly at Jack, a bewildered expression on her face.

"Oh my God," Jack mumbled.

Tess said something to Dick and then sashayed back to the table, stopping several times as people came over to congratulate her on the highest-earning item of the evening and to thank her for supporting the cause. When she finally made it back to the table, Jack rose and pulled out her chair. She sat down, turned to him, and quietly said, "Dick just said the strangest thing to me."

Jack's face fell.

"He congratulated me on having the backbone to make you sign a prenup. Why on earth would he say something like that?"

"Sweetheart, I'm so sorry you found out like this. Before we got married, your lawyers drew up a prenup. I found out and signed it. You weren't meant to ever know about it."

"What?" she asked, shock in her eyes.

"Sweetheart, it's not even legally binding without your signature, but I wanted you to have it in case you ever wanted it."

Her eyes fell to her lap and she shook her head, visibly trying to process what she had heard. When she looked up, her eyes went to Omar like a laser. "What did you do?" she demanded.

"Butterfly, please. Jack found out about it and asked me directly. I couldn't very well lie."

"But you could have respected my wishes."

"Butterfly, please, it was an impossible situation. We had your best interest at heart."

"My best interest? I can't believe you, either of you," she said, turning to Jack, tears in her eyes.

"Sweetheart, please…"

"Take me home," she said, a hot tear rolling down her cheek.

Jack just looked at her, a pained expression on his face.

"Now," she said softly, wiping away more tears.

CHAPTER 5

The ride home was silent and tense. As they walked into their home, Tess dropped her clutch on the kitchen counter and headed to their bedroom, Jack following behind. She sat at her vanity and removed her shoes and jewelry. When she took off her heart locket, she held it in her open palm, gazing down at it. "Tess," Jack said softly.

She opened her jewelry box, dropped the necklace in its usual spot, and stood up. Turning her back toward him, she said, "Please unzip me."

He gently unzipped her gown and placed his hands on her shoulders.

"Tess, we need to talk. How about I make us some tea?"

She held her gown up against her body, softly said, "Fine. I need to get out of this first," and scurried to the bathroom.

Ten minutes later, she meandered into the kitchen in pajamas. Jack was sitting on a stool at the counter, having changed into sweatpants and a T-shirt. "I made chamomile," he said, gesturing to the mugs. She sat down beside him, staring at her mug and slowly dunking her teabag up and down.

He put his hand on her wrist and she let go of the teabag string. "Tess, please talk to me. Let me try to explain."

She turned to him and asked, "What happened between Omar and Raj tonight?"

He looked surprised. "Uh, Raj accused him, well, us really, of treating you like a child."

Tess sighed loudly.

"He told Omar about the ultimatum and that you had broken up with him over it. Omar was surprised. He thought Raj was the one to end things."

"He was," Tess said. "He knew I'd never give in to his demand. It was his way of pushing me to end it. At the time, I was relieved."

"Why? You said he was a good guy."

"You spent years avoiding relationships, having one-night stands but not really dating because your job didn't allow it. I was the opposite. I dated countless men from all walks of life, all briefly, and I always ended it for the same reason: I didn't love them. Raj was the loveliest man I had ever been with, and one of the only ones who didn't give a lick that I was Tess Lee. It killed me that I couldn't love him. I thought there was something wrong with me. I believed so fully in romantic love, yet I never fell in love, not until you. When we met, I realized there wasn't anything wrong with me—I just hadn't met the right person." She rested her forehead in her hand.

"Sweetheart, you look sad."

She was silent. Eventually, in a quiet voice, she said, "You broke my heart. Yes, I'm sad. I'm also angry at you, Jack. It's a horrible feeling and I'm trying to get used to it." He massaged her hand and she looked at him. "Do you know that in over four years, I have never once been mad at you? Not once. Not for a single second of our entire relationship."

"I know baby. I'm so sorry that you found out about this, and worst of all, that you found out from that blowhard."

She raised her eyebrows. "*That's* what you're sorry for? That I found out you lied to me? That I found out from that asshole? What does any of that matter?" She shook her head, took a long breath, and continued, "How about being sorry for going behind my back, not respecting my wishes, betraying me, and breaking our trust? How about being sorry for starting our marriage with a secret? How about being sorry for dragging Omar into it and damaging the trust he and I share?"

"Tess, please don't read into this. I was only trying to do the honorable thing. It's not even legally valid without your signature. I signed it so that if you ever wanted out, you wouldn't have to worry about anything."

"Worry about money? My God, Jack, do you know me at all? You think that if we had a catastrophic problem in our relationship, I would be thinking about our finances? The fact that you were planning for the possibility, that you didn't have faith we would always be together, I don't even know how to respond to that. It's devastating," she said, shaking her head and looking down.

"Sweetheart, I was only trying to protect you. I promise you that I knew I'd never leave you, but I wanted you to have the freedom to do as you pleased. I hoped you'd be with me forever but because it was your choice, not because you were stuck. We had only known each other for four weeks, when we got married, and…"

"What does it matter how long we knew each other? When we decided to get married, I thought it was because we loved each other completely and wanted to share the rest of our lives. I knew how I felt about you after our first night together. Did you really not know, even at our wedding?"

"No, baby. Of course I knew. I loved you with my whole heart, then, now, every moment in between, and forever. But ours wasn't the typical financial situation most newlyweds have. You had built an empire worth over half a billion dollars. You did that yourself, with your talent, your intelligence, your blood, sweat, and tears. The night I signed the stupid thing, you had made that massive donation to pediatric cancer research in Gracie's name. It was the most loving and generous thing anyone had ever done for me. I was only trying to be worthy."

"Jack, you already were." She paused for a moment to gather her thoughts. "I believe you were trying to do what you thought was right. The fact that you can't see how that makes me feel, even now, that you're rationalizing what you did, makes me think that you don't understand me."

He reached for her hand. "Sweetheart, I can see how upset you are, but if you know I was only trying to protect you, then…"

She leapt up and hollered, "Because that's the problem! You don't respect me. You look at me like some fragile, defenseless thing in need of your help. You and Omar both. I don't want your protection; I want your love."

"I do love you. People who love each other protect each other. It's natural."

"But Jack, you were trying to protect me from my own judgment. You didn't trust me to look out for myself. Do you realize how hurtful that is? Do you think I built the net worth you mentioned by being stupid or naïve? Do you understand why I always wanted to own the rights to all my books, even back in the beginning when I had nothing and was offered millions to sell those rights? Do you know the reason? It was because I didn't want men controlling me. I wanted to be in charge of my own destiny. And now you, the man I love and trust most in the world, has taken a piece of that from me. And your only response is that you're sorry I found out."

"Tess…"

She put her hand up and, in a calmer voice, said, "Please let me finish."

He nodded.

"What really hurts me is not only that you lied to me, that you were willing to compromise the trust we have between us, but that you didn't respect me enough to honor my wishes. Did it ever occur to you that I had valid reasons for not wanting you to sign that thing? Maybe I wanted our marriage to be based on equality, and that includes finances. Maybe I didn't want to make it easier for either of us to ever leave, to ever decide we weren't worth fighting for. Maybe I needed to know that even if the worst did happen, it wouldn't have been because I hadn't tried my hardest to make our marriage work. Maybe giving myself entirely to someone for the first time in my life was truly important to me, and that included everything I have and all that I am. Maybe after having no real family in my life, knowing with certainty that you were my forever family was worth more to me than any amount of money. You see, Jack, maybe I had a whole host of reasons, but you never bothered to consider that. You inserted your own judgment over mine. To you, I guess I was just a silly girl in love who needed to be protected, even from myself. But I wanted us to have a certain kind of marriage. It was a considered decision and one I've never regretted."

He stood up and put his arms around her. She tried to push him away. He whispered, "Please, sweetheart. Just let me hold you for a minute so you can feel how much I love you." She relented and he held her closely, rubbing her back and stroking her hair. "I'm so sorry, Tess. I promise I didn't mean it that way. I do respect you, more than anyone. I'm in awe of you. I was trying to give you freedom, not take it from you. It was such a mistake."

She pulled back, tears in her eyes. "Do you have any idea what our marriage means to me?"

He used his thumbs to wipe away her tears. "Of course. I see it in your eyes when we make love. I hear it in your voice when you say good morning. I feel it in your touch. Sweetheart, our marriage is everything to me, too."

"There's nothing without trust, Jack. What you did hurt me."

"I'm so sorry."

"I know you're a good man and that you were only doing what you thought was honorable, but I would never go behind your back, for anything, ever. We need to have complete trust."

"I know, baby, and I promise it will never happen again. I don't ever want to make you look at me again the way you have tonight. I won't forget this."

He brushed the side of her face, leaned forward, and touched his lips to hers.

She pulled away. "Jack, I need some time. I'm upset."

Before he could respond, Tess's phone rang. "That's strange, it's so late," she said. She opened her purse and retrieved the phone. "Clay's calling."

"Hello... What? ... Oh my God, is he okay? ... How did this happen? ... We're on our way."

"Sweetheart, what's wrong?" Jack asked.

She burst into tears. "Omar was attacked. It was some sort of hate crime. He's in the hospital."

***

Jack and Tess were standing at the front desk in the emergency room, trying to find out where Omar was, when Clay came to get them. He was still in his tuxedo but was a mess.

"Oh, Clay," Tess said, hugging him tightly. He squeezed her like he was never going to let go. When they eventually parted, Tess asked, "How is he?"

"He has a black eye, a split lip, and two broken ribs. They knocked him to the ground and were kicking him. I'm surprised he's not bleeding internally," he said, tears starting to fall from his eyes. He sniffled and continued, "They've given him something for the pain, so he's in better spirits. He'll be so happy to see you."

"What on earth happened?" Tess asked.

"On the way home, we stopped at the drugstore. We had been quarreling and wanted to have a chat and a midnight snack, so he ran in to get some ice cream. I waited in the car, which I shouldn't have done, but…"

Tess put her hand on his arm. "There's no way you could have known this would happen. This isn't your fault, Clay."

"There were a couple of young white guys in the store. They started harassing him, calling him a terrorist, a suicide bomber, and other racist slurs, and telling him to go back to where he came from. He tried to ignore them, but they followed him out of the store. They just started wailing on him. Don't they see they're the terrorists?"

"It makes me sick," Jack said. "I spent decades fighting actual terrorists. People I know have given their lives to battle real threats, and these punks go after law-abiding citizens."

"If bystanders hadn't started screaming, they would have killed him. The police said they were surprised he wasn't in worse shape. Can you imagine?" Clay choked up. "That's what they said."

"Can we see him?" Tess asked.

"Follow me. You can't stay long. They're preparing to discharge him soon," Clay said, leading them to the far corner of the room. He pulled back a paper curtain to reveal Omar lying in a rolling bed, his chest bandaged, his face swollen and bruised, an intravenous drip attached to his arm.

When Tess saw him, she gasped softly.

"That bad, Butterfly? Am I no longer handsome?"

She sat on the edge of the bed, smiled dimly, and said, "Well, to be fair, you weren't that handsome to begin with."

He laughed and then made a pained face. "That's the thing about broken ribs. They've taken my looks and my humor. It's unconscionable."

"How are you feeling?" she asked, holding his hand.

"Well, the morphine drip is lovely. One could get used to this."

"That's the spirit," she said. "Perhaps you can get a nice new addiction out of this, make yourself more interesting."

"Butterfly, I know you're angry with me about earlier, and…"

"Don't be silly. None of that matters now," she said, shaking her head and crinkling her nose. "I love you beyond measure. Clay and I are going to take very good care of you. We'll spoil you rotten, which I'm sure you'll have fun abusing."

He smiled.

She squeezed his hand. "Please just rest and heal. I'll come see you tomorrow. I'm going to spend so much time at your place, Clay will go out of his mind. Since you can't laugh, I'm thinking a marathon of slasher films is in our future."

He smiled again and squeezed her hand. "I love you, Butterfly."

"I love you more," she said.

"I hope you feel better soon," Jack said. "Let me know if I can help."

"I'll be right back, love," Clay said.

Clay walked them to the front door. Tess embraced him. "I'll call first thing in the morning and I'll be over whenever it's good for you. I'll have food for the week delivered so you won't have to worry about that."

"Thank you. I'm going to take some time off," he replied.

"Whenever you have to go back to work, I'll be there. I'll come over every day to care for him. I can hire a nighttime nurse if you like. Anything you both need."

"Thank you, Tess. I love you. We both do. I'll see you tomorrow."

They all said goodbye and Tess and Jack left. As soon as they got outside, Tess doubled over and exploded into tears, sobbing uncontrollably. Jack put his hand on her back. "It's okay, sweetheart. He'll be okay."

Eventually she looked up, her face a wet, red mess. "I can't believe anyone would do this to him," she cried.

"I know. It's disgusting."

"I can hardly breathe," she said, gasping for air.

He continued rubbing her back. "It's okay baby, just breathe. Just breathe. He's tough and he has Clay. He has us. It's horrible, but he'll be okay."

Once she calmed down, she looked at him with tearful eyes, and softly said, "I've had my heart broken twice tonight. And the worst part is I don't have you."

"You do have me. Sweetheart, you always have me," he said, putting his arms around her.

***

Tess gazed out the car window, silent tears running down her face the entire way home. No words were spoken. Jack opened the front door and she passed through, shuffling to their bedroom. "I need to clean up," she sniffled quietly, heading into their bathroom. When she emerged a few minutes later in pajamas, Jack was waiting for her by the door.

"Hey, come here," he said softly, opening his arms.

She burst into tears, dropping her face into her hands.

"Oh, sweetheart," he said, throwing his arms around her. "He'll be okay. Everything will be okay."

After a moment passed, she stopped crying. She pulled her head back to look at him. He gently brushed the hair out of her face and whispered, "I love you so much."

He leaned forward and kissed her lightly. They paused to look at each other. He ran his fingertips along her cheek. They began kissing, softly. Jack pulled his shirt off and Tess followed suit, pulling off her clothes. They stumbled to the bed. Soon they were making love tenderly, their eyes locked. After, they lay kissing and touching each other's faces.

"Tess, I love you with my whole heart."

"I love you, too."

"I always want to know what's going on in your mind. Did you know that whenever you're sad, when we make love, you pull me on top of you? It's this thing you do. And the way you look at me, I can't describe it."

"Jack, do you remember the night you proposed?"

"Yes."

"What do you remember?"

"I remember everything. We were at Shelby's with the gang and Omar was pressuring you to close that entertainment deal. When you did, you said that selling your work was like selling a piece of your soul. They all thought you were joking, but I knew you weren't. We went to speak privately, and you asked if I thought it was possible for two people to know each other completely. I said yes."

She smiled and ran her fingers against his temple.

"Then 'All of Me' came on, our song, and we danced, melting into each other. I didn't think it was possible to love you more than I did in that moment, but when we left there was that homeless man, Henry. It wasn't just that you spoke with him and gave him money, it was *the way* you spoke with him, *the way* you held his hands. I had never witnessed such kindness. You were like an angel. It was the opposite of almost everything else I'd seen in my life. I wanted to be around your goodness forever. Then you gave him your scarf. When we got into the car and I saw him wrapping it around his neck, I knew that if I was somehow lucky enough that you'd want me, I'd never let you go."

She leaned forward and pressed her mouth to his.

"By the time we got to your place, I couldn't wait to be with you. We couldn't even make it to the pillows. I laid you down across the bed because I just had to have you."

"Jack, when we were making love that night, I looked at your body and your face above me. I had never felt so safe or happy in my entire life. In that moment, it was like nothing bad had ever happened to me, like nothing at all had ever happened before you. Then you asked me to marry you and I felt so lucky because I knew I would get to feel that way for the rest of my life. When I think about us, about my feelings for you, that's the moment I picture. Your beautiful face over mine, it's my safest place."

"That's how I feel every time I look into your beautiful, brown eyes. Like it's the safest, most loving place in the world. The only place I want to live."

She looked down.

"What is it, baby?" he asked, putting his hand on her cheek.

"This is going to sound ridiculous, but I've always felt that our relationship is perfect. I know people say that no marriage is perfect, but I've always felt ours truly is. What we have means everything to me."

"To me too," he said.

"I married you with an open heart. I thought that we both meant it forever."

"Tess, I promised you my whole heart forever, and that's exactly what I meant. I would never leave you."

"Then why'd you sign that paper?"

"So you'd always know how much I love you just as you are, as you truly are. Sweetheart, when you were growing up, those men took things from you that should never be taken from anyone. You had no control. I wanted you to live the rest of your life with the freedom to make your own choices, to be the one in control. I promise that my heart was in the right place. I would never knowingly do anything to hurt you." He stroked her hair. "I'm sorry that I hadn't considered any of the things you said tonight. If I had, I wouldn't have signed the paper. I was only trying to love and protect you the best I knew how." He brushed the side of her face. "I'm so sorry. I was wrong. Please, baby. I love you so much."

"Jack, the closeness between us, it means so much to me. Like you said earlier tonight, the way we see each other is everything. We trust each other so deeply. Please promise you won't ever make me question that trust again."

"I promise."

"I love you," she said.

He pulled her face to him and touched the tip of his nose to the tip of hers.

"Will you hold me close to you until I fall asleep? I just want to feel your arms."

"Come here," he said. She turned around and burrowed into him. He put his arm over her, pulling her firmly to his body. "Try to get some sleep, sweetheart. I love you. Omar will be all right. We will be all right. Everyone will be all right."

"I hope so."

***

The next day, after arranging a food delivery service and a nighttime nurse, Tess headed to visit Omar with a box of pastries in hand. She sat on the edge of his bed, smiling at him.

"I would have baked something myself, but I didn't want to miss a minute with you."

"I would have waited if you had stopped by the White House to bake something with the president, your other BFF. How many people can say the leader of the free world made them a get well treat?"

Tess laughed. "Kate's traveling for some international meetings, but when she's back in DC, I'll pop by the White House and we'll whip you up something special. In the meantime, I went to the best bakery in town."

"Wow, you got all my favorites," Omar said, peeking into the box. "You're going to make me fat. I won't be working out for a while."

"You'll still be gorgeous. Plump and soft and gorgeous. I thought you could use a treat."

"He definitely could. Which one do you want? I'll fix you a plate and make some tea while you visit," Clay said.

"That one," Omar said, pointing. Clay took the box and left.

"I know you're trying to put on a happy face, Butterfly, but I can see it in your eyes. I must look awful."

She smiled, crinkled her nose, and shook her head as tears filled her eyes. "I just hate seeing you hurt," she said, almost inaudibly. "I'm so sorry this happened to you, Omar. I don't even have the words, and you know that's not like me."

He took her hand. "I know and I love you."

"Are you in terrible pain?" she asked.

"I've felt better, but the bruises will heal. The rest of it is trickier."

"I know. The residue of the violence, of the violation, the fear of the next time, and the anger, to some extent, always remain."

"I wish you didn't understand that so well, Butterfly."

"It must have been terrifying."

"I've been living in this body my whole life, so unfortunately, hate is nothing new to me, but it doesn't make it any less frightening or painful."

"I'm so sorry. I know we can't take any of it away, but you have me and you have Clay, and of course Jack too. We'll do anything for you."

"I know and I'm grateful. It's strange because of course I would never want anyone else to feel what I've had to feel, especially Clay, and yet, it's helpful that he truly understands. As a Black man, he's been dealing with racism and hatred his whole life too. He understands all the dimensions of what I'm going through."

"Last night, I was thinking about the night I met Jack. I don't know if you remember, I was supposed to meet you and Clay at that bar, but you canceled last minute."

"I remember. Clay was pulled over for being Black when he was leaving the hospital after working a hellacious shift. You told me to stay with him to help him process it. The one glorious thing to come out of that night was you meeting the love of your life. I can't imagine you without Jack."

"Me either." She smiled faintly. "It saddens me to think there was such darkness in your life that night, and now again, and all the other times. Violence is horrific. There are some things in this world I will never understand."

"Me either. But at least we have each other," he said.

She squeezed his hand. "Always."

Clay walked in and handed them each a plate. "Tess, I know you don't normally eat sweets, but I picked something I thought you'd enjoy, just in case. I'll be back in a moment with the tea."

"I think today I'll make an exception, thank you. We could all use a little sweetness," she said, picking up the pastry and taking a big bite.

Omar smiled.

CHAPTER 6

Joe, Bobby, Omar, and Clay were catching up when Tess and Jack arrived at Shelby's.

"Hey guys," Jack said as they sat down.

"We took the liberty of ordering you drinks," Omar said.

"Thanks," Jack replied, raising his beer bottle and clinking it to Tess's sparkling water.

"Where are Gina and Luciana?" Tess asked.

"Gina didn't want to leave Rob. Plus, she's wiped. She told me to go without her and asked me to say hello to everyone," Bobby said, taking a swig of beer.

"Luciana's working on a new piece for her upcoming show. She couldn't leave it," Joe said.

"Ah, I understand. When you're in the flow, you have to run with it. Inspiration doesn't oblige our schedules," Tess said.

"So I'm learning," Joe said. "The piece she's working on is wonderful. And she's looking forward to when the four of us can get together again to go salsa dancing."

Tess smiled. "Well, all the better for me. It's not every day I get five handsome men all to myself."

Jack put his arm around her and pecked her on the cheek. She leaned into him.

"Omar, I'm so happy to see you back to your old self. Honestly, I could cry," Tess said.

"Well, control yourself, we don't need you causing a scene," he replied with a laugh. "Seriously, Butterfly, you were so sweet to visit me every day during my recovery. I did enjoy our movie marathons."

Tess smiled.

"Did they ever find the guys who assaulted you?" Bobby asked.

Omar shook his head. "It's been six weeks, so I'm sure you know the chances are slim."

"Sometimes these punks never get caught," Bobby said.

"Thank goodness you're well. That's what really matters," Tess said. "I love you to bits."

"Good, because there's something I wanted to talk to you about. Butterfly, your *Vogue* cover story is causing quite the stir. It's their bestselling issue in years."

"Don't remind me. Jack and I have hardly been able to leave the house. People are very kind, but it's overwhelming. Not to mention all the pointing and whispering. We've been hibernating since it hit newsstands. It's reminded me why I value my privacy."

"That bad?" Bobby asked.

Jack sighed. "Let's just say she's been getting a lot of unwanted attention. I thought I knew the drill, but since that magazine came out, it's been off the charts. Look over there," he said, gesturing toward the bar. "That group hasn't stopped staring since we walked in."

Tess craned her neck to look up at him and said, "Just ignore them, baby. But I warned you we should have left the country when it hit."

"Well, Butterfly, you've refused to do television and magazines for the last five years. People were just dying for their dose of Tess Lee."

Tess rolled her eyes.

"Jack, you should have seen what it was like back when she was living in LA, doing the full media circus thing for years. She couldn't go anywhere without private security and a driver," Omar said.

"Hey, I'm all for a driver," Jack said with a chuckle.

"God, she really is dreadful. Total menace," Omar added.

Tess nudged Jack in the shoulder and flung a pretzel at Omar. Everyone laughed and Tess said, "As you'll recall, I didn't enjoy that time in my life. You know I always wanted to simply write my books, try to give back, and live a private existence. The whole fame thing is absurd. For goodness' sake, I'm a writer, not a movie star."

"Jack may kick my ass, but let me just say—holy cow, you're smoking in that magazine," Bobby said.

Jack shot him a look.

"Dude, she's really hot, insanely hot. It's an undeniable fact," he said, taking a swill of his beer. "Gina bought like ten copies of the magazine. That one picture in the strapless dress where you're sitting on the desk with one leg hanging down the side, hunched over with your head on your other knee, my eyes nearly popped out of my head. Were you wearing body glitter? Your skin looked so..."

"Hey now, that's my wife," Jack said playfully.

Bobby shrugged.

"You do look spectacular, Butterfly."

"I especially liked the one of you in the men's suit, standing in front of that huge pile of books. You looked powerful," Clay said.

"Other than the cover, my favorite is the one where she's sitting on our window seat, gazing outside, her book on her lap," Jack said.

Tess craned her neck and kissed him softly. "You like that one because it's the closest to something real."

He kissed her again.

"Tess, the pictures are stunning. I confess to stopping in my tracks when I saw the cover," Joe said. "But the essay you wrote was powerful and inspiring. Your perspective on the rights of artists and the treatment of women's work is something people need to hear and there's no one better equipped to speak to those issues than you. I couldn't have been more impressed."

"Me either," Jack said, raising his beer bottle.

"You're all very sweet. The essay was the reason I agreed to do it. I had some things to say. The photos were the price to pay to say them. Once the magazine lands in recycling bins, hopefully people will start to forget a bit and life can go back to normal."

"Butterfly, your life has never been normal."

"Well, normal-ish," she conceded.

"Butterfly, at the risk of you disowning me, there's something I need to run by you. I know you hate mixing business and pleasure, but I thought perhaps having your friends here might help. When you see their reactions, perhaps..."

"Out with it already. I can tell from the drawn-out preface that I'm not going to like this."

"You're right," Clay said.

Omar shot him a look. "You're not helping."

"I'm helping Tess," Clay replied.

"That bad?" Tess asked playfully.

"Oh, you'll see," Clay said.

"Come on, out with it, Omar," Tess cajoled.

"Well, since the magazine came out, we've been inundated with requests from late-night TV, the morning talk shows, magazines, and so on."

"Yes, and as I've already made clear, I'm not living that life again. The *Vogue* spread was a one-time thing so I could get a message out. That's all."

"Yes, Butterfly, but as has always been the case with you, whenever you do press, book sales soar and entertainment deals start rolling in. The team thinks you should at least consider the business side."

"I'm sorry, but is anyone starving? We sell plenty of books without me parading around in designer clothes or whoring myself on late-night TV."

"Funny you should say whoring," Clay said.

Omar shot him a look. "Yes, I know, Butterfly. But there's one offer that came in that everyone hopes you'll at least consider. It would be wonderful for attracting younger readers who are interested in your work and of course your message. It's very cool, so cool, in fact, that I wanted our friends here. When you see their reactions, you may think about it differently."

"Sounds to me like you wanted witnesses so I couldn't yell at you."

"Well, there is that too," Omar said, smiling. "Anyway, *Rolling Stone* wants you for a cover story. Butterfly, it would be historic."

"Wow, that's awesome," Bobby said.

"Tess, I've always thought we aren't nearly cool enough to hang out with you. I think this proves it," Joe said.

Tess turned to Jack, who said, "It's very flattering, sweetheart. Further proof that I'm the luckiest guy on this planet. But after what I've seen since *Vogue* came out, I don't want you to put yourself in that position if you don't want to do it. If you do, of course I'll support you every way I can. I'm getting pretty good at being your bodyguard."

She smiled and stroked his cheek. "You're the best, and having the guarantee that you'd be nearby all the time would be the one thing that would make it worth it."

"Sweetheart, you already have that."

"Perhaps this isn't the best time since you're feeling so exposed right now, but I do think you should consider it," Omar said.

"You haven't told her everything," Clay said. He looked at Tess and Jack and sarcastically said, "You two will *love* this."

Omar sighed. "Well, this is just one idea they had, mind you. They were thinking for the cover you could be, very tastefully of course, well... topless."

Bobby choked on his beer and some came shooting out of his mouth.

"What?!" Jack bellowed.

Omar continued, "Of course with your long, fabulous hair covering your..."

"My what, Omar? Finish that sentence. I dare you," Tess said.

"I told you," Clay said. "He's gone from being your best friend to your pimp."

"You're not helping," Omar said.

"Uh, I have a pretty strong *no* reaction to that," Jack said.

"Oh, that's nothing. You should have heard what *Maxim* wanted her to do," Omar muttered.

Tess giggled. "As if I would ever. I'm sorry, Omar, have we met? Is there any reality in which you think I would do this? First of all, I hate PR. Standing up for values I believe in is one thing, and I've sacrificed parts of myself for that over and over again. But doing something just to bolster my celebrity, which I never wanted in the first place, big fat *no*. Second, you know how I feel about the objectification of women. My goodness, did you even read my *Vogue* essay?"

"Yes, Butterfly, I know. Of course I immediately and decisively nixed it, along with some other ideas they had."

"Such as?"

"Oh, well, a pencil in your mouth. That sort of thing."

She shook her head. "Unbelievable. What is it with men and oral fixations?"

All the guys looked down and then burst into laughter. Tess laughed too.

"I know you're not taking this seriously, but please hear me out," Omar continued.

She raised her eyebrows impatiently.

"Of course I knew none of those ideas were acceptable. I also knew you'd never do PR for PR's sake. I brainstormed and came up with something you might find exciting. The magazine ate it up. The editor practically had an orgasm."

"I hope it doesn't involve my wife taking her clothes off," Jack said.

"It doesn't. Butterfly, everyone knows about your close friendship with Mick. Although you two have never spoken publicly about your relationship, there's quite a bit of interest in how two huge stars from such different art forms have quietly been friends for twenty years."

"Mick and I don't talk about it because it's private, like all my relationships."

"Yes, but my idea was this: you and Mick do the cover and photo spread together, and inside you'll interview each other, like a conversation. You can make the whole thing about art—from the creative process to artists' rights. You could even talk about the importance of libraries. I know you two speak about that stuff all the time. It would just be a public version of that conversation, which you two would personally curate. You'd have complete control. It would be a way to turn this opportunity into something completely on-message. It will be about artists, not you. Plus, we both know you'd have oodles of fun doing this with Mick."

"That's it, we're *definitely* not cool enough to hang out with you," Bobby said.

"Definitely," Joe added.

Jack rubbed Tess's arm. "Sweetheart, what do you think?"

"I think Mick will have as little interest in this as I do," she replied.

"I already called him. He wanted to contact you, but I asked him to give me a chance to ease you into the idea. We both know how you can be."

She shot him the side-eye.

"Butterfly, Mick is in. He said he'd love to do it and he has his own reasons, which you'd probably understand better than anyone.

He even sent me loads of pictures from the photo shoots you two have done, to remind you how much fun you always have together. Here," he said, sliding his phone across the table.

"You've done photo shoots with him before?" Jack asked.

"No, not really. When they're on tour and I visit them backstage, he always has their photographer take a ton of shots of us, mostly black and white. They're just for his personal collection. They've never been made public."

"Can I see?" Jack asked.

"Yeah, we all want to see," Bobby added enthusiastically.

"Suit yourselves," she said, passing the phone with a shrug.

"He really likes to lick the side of your face, huh?" Jack said, scrolling through the photos.

Tess giggled. "It's kind of his thing."

"I like this one, where he's sitting at your feet. You can see how close you two are by the way you look at each other," Jack said.

Tess smiled. "I only took these because they were private, just goofing off with a friend."

"Let me see," Bobby said.

Jack handed him the phone. His eyes were like saucers as he swiped through the pictures.

"Butterfly, will you think about it? Mick is expecting to hear from you either way."

"No time like the present. He's nocturnal, after all. If you all don't mind, I'll FaceTime him and see what he *really* thinks."

"Do we mind? Are you kidding?" Bobby asked.

Tess giggled and dialed Mick's number.

"Hello, darling. I thought I'd hear from you," Mick said.

"I'm in a bar with Jack, Omar, and a few of our friends you met at our wedding. I'm going to prop the phone up on a pretzel basket."

Mick laughed. "Oh darling, you're so wonderfully American. Hello, everyone."

"Hi," they all said.

Mick continued, "I've been meaning to call you. Your *Vogue* cover was heart-stopping. Just when I think you can't get more beautiful. The glamour shot on the cover; your face, your big, brown eyes looking as if you're a heartbeat away from tears. It's the most vulnerable, gorgeous cover image I've ever seen. Holy shit. Someday you'll have to tell me what you were thinking of when they shot that. The essay—spot on. What you said about artists owning the rights to their work and deciding how it should be made available, I was cheering. Well done."

"Thank you. I sacrificed myself for the cover to write the essay."

"And now they're trying to convince you to do it again," he said.

"Exactly."

"Vultures," Mick said, breaking out into hearty laughter. "Darling, do you remember what you said to me when we first met?"

"Yes."

"Well, I'm going to say it to you now because I think we'd have a ball doing this together. I asked you if by chasing freedom we ended up creating another kind of cage, code for fame. I'll never forget your reply. You said, 'It doesn't matter, because if you're surrounded by light, you won't see the bars.' Darling, there's no one with more light around them than you. You positively glow."

Tess smiled. "I see Omar has worked on you."

"Perhaps, but he didn't have to try very hard. I've always wanted to collaborate. This is our chance. We can piggyback on the momentum of your essay. Don't worry, we'll put our legal teams to good use and have them place a stranglehold around the mag. It will be our words and only images that meet our approval."

"Did Omar tell you that they wanted me to be topless on the cover?"

"Yes, and darling, I have to say, we all want that," he replied, breaking out into laughter again.

"You can imagine Jack's reaction."

"Darling, if there weren't an ocean between us, I'd have been too afraid to say it."

Tess smirked.

"I'm only teasing. So my darling, what do you think?" Mick asked.

"Tell me why you want to do this."

"You know our favorite lyric? Even Tom didn't understand what we heard in those words. No one does, only the two of us. Those words, that's why."

She smiled, said, "I understand," and looked at Jack.

"Sweetheart, it's up to you. It does seem like it would be something special. We can travel when it comes out to avoid the circus, maybe go to our place in Hawaii. No one bothers you there. I'll do my best to shield you from the attention."

"It would be the bloody story of the decade," Mick said. "We can stand up for artists in a big, splashy way that no one can ignore. Think of this title: Mick and Tess on Friendship, Fame, and the Fight for Artists' Rights."

Tess thought about it for a minute and said, "One condition: you and I wear the same wardrobe."

Mick laughed. "Well, I have no problem going shirtless, as you know."

Tess giggled.

"How about black leather pants and tank tops so Jack doesn't kill me? We can have them do the whole spread in black and white, even the cover."

Tess looked around the table. Everyone was nodding. Jack dropped a kiss in her hair.

"Okay, I'm in. Let's have our teams set it up. If nothing else, it'll be a good excuse to see you."

"Can't wait. They want to fast-track it, and as it turns out, I'm going to be in New York in two weeks. Can you meet me there? We can lock ourselves away in a hotel suite to hammer out the piece and have them shoot it at their studio in the city. I may be able to get Annie to do it."

"Jack and I never spend a night apart," she said.

"He's a lucky man," Mick replied.

Tess turned to Jack. "I can go with you," he said, caressing her arm.

"Okay. Let's do it. I'll get my team started on the arrangements," Tess said.

"Splendid. Now darling, I must go. I think there's a party going on at my place and I should probably make an appearance."

She giggled and said, "Love you."

"Love you. Bye."

After hanging up, she burrowed into Jack.

"I should have Mick do all my negotiating," Omar said. "Seems he knows just what to say. I thought this would take weeks."

"What have I gotten myself into?"

"Tess, what's the lyric he was talking about?" Bobby asked.

She smiled. "Peace in the valley. It's from a Tom Petty song. It's just our way of saying we will stay calm and centered, no matter the chaos surrounding us."

Jack squeezed her and said, "Mick was right about the *Vogue* cover shot. It's so beautiful, like nothing I've seen before. What were you thinking about?"

She turned to look at him. "You. I was thinking about how much I love you."

He leaned forward and pressed his lips lightly to hers. Just then, a slow song came on and he asked, "Sweetheart, how about a dance?"

"Absolutely."

They walked onto the dance floor, holding each other tightly. "Do you think I'm crazy? I mean, you know what it's been like recently."

"It'll all be okay, baby. I think you'll have fun and you'll get to spread your message even further. I promise I'll take care of everything else. I'm curious—why'd you say yes?"

She turned and looked back at the table, Omar and her friends all laughing and having a good time. She gazed into Jack's eyes. "I guess I'm just in a place of gratitude and want to make the most of things. Omar's okay now after that nightmare. You and I survived our first argument, and we're stronger than ever. Maybe the storm cloud has lifted."

"Nothing but lightness ahead," he whispered.

He kissed her softly and they continued to dance, running their hands through each other's hair, pressing their bodies close together, content in their love and the belief that the darkness had passed.

CHAPTER 7

"Oh my God, that was so much fun," Tess said as she and Jack dropped down into their seats.

"I never thought I'd see the day—Jack salsa dancing," Bobby said with a chuckle.

"It shows you how far a man will go to keep his wife happy," Jack said.

"Come on, you had fun, baby," Tess said, touching his arm. "You're getting pretty good, too."

"You are," Luciana agreed.

"I blame you for this," Jack said to Luciana, taking a sip of his beer. "Actually, Joe, it's your fault. If you hadn't started coming here with Luciana, I wouldn't be here."

Joe laughed. "There's no point in fighting it. When a beautiful woman asks you for something, just do it."

Luciana leaned over and pecked him on the cheek.

"I'm just glad Gina took Rob to visit her grandparents because there's no way I'd go out there, and you know she'd hassle me," Bobby said.

"You should give it a try some time," Tess said. "It's very sexy."

"Is it?" Jack asked, leaning over and kissing her.

"Sure is," she replied, stroking the side of his face.

"Hawaii must have been great for you guys. You seem happier than ever, which I didn't think was possible," Bobby said.

Jack leaned back in his chair. "Maui is always great. Honestly, I just wanted to get Tess away from all the madness. When that *Rolling Stone* issue came out, I knew the heat would be cranked way up. We're lucky we had somewhere secluded to escape to."

"Amazing that it was only two months ago that we were talking about it at Shelby's. Has it been crazy?" Joe asked.

Tess nodded. "This is the first time I've left the house without a baseball cap. Between *Vogue* and the spread with Mick, things are too dialed up for my taste."

"Not to mention all the tabloids," Jack said. "I told you you'd cause a stir by walking through Central Park with Mick."

"We needed some fresh air and inspiration. We were wearing sunglasses and hats," Tess replied.

"If you hadn't stopped to give money to every homeless person you saw, you might not have been recognized," he said, massaging her hand.

She shrugged.

Jack turned to the group. "The breakdancing caused it to spiral out of control. There were these street performers, and of course Tess stopped to join in, and then Mick got going. They each have boundless energy, but when they're together, forget about it. You should have seen the crowd that formed, everyone filming them. Then the paps showed up. Thank God we had security with us. It wasn't easy getting them back to the hotel."

"Well, I wasn't happy to see it splashed across all the tabloids, but it sure was fun," Tess admitted.

"It was like you and Mick didn't even notice the commotion around you," Jack said.

"We didn't. We were surrounded by light."

Jack leaned over and kissed her softly.

"Oh trust me, we saw all of it. Gina bought like every magazine and we watched so many of the videos on YouTube," Bobby said. "Tess, that's how we learned you're secretly married to Mick, and Jack is just your bodyguard," he said, bursting into laughter.

Jack laughed. "I've never gotten so many phone calls from my family before, asking questions."

Tess giggled.

"If it's any consolation, the *Rolling Stone* issue was incredible. I was blown away," Joe said.

"Seriously, I showed it to everyone I know," Bobby added. "The photos were awesome. Love the black and white. The cover shot, with your arms on each other's shoulders, *damn*. The ones in movement, especially the one of you two suspended in air with your hair whipping around, that was so freaking cool. And the one of you sitting with Mick's head in your lap was super sweet. You guys look so happy, like you were having the time of your lives."

"They were," Jack said. "They decided ahead of time exactly what they wanted for the photographs, starting with the high energy pics. The crew tried to match their energy. Mick is so funny. When they started the shoot, he put the soundtrack to *Fame* on as a joke. You should have seen the two of them laughing hysterically, him picking her up, them dancing and jumping. All the joy came through in the pictures. The closeness they share, too. When they did the intimate beauty shots at the end of the day, you could hear a pin drop. Omar told me I was in for a treat, and he was right. He said, 'Some stars just shine brighter together.' Everyone on the set told me it was the most magical job they'd ever worked."

Tess smiled. "It was a good time. Too bad the whole world had to be in on it."

"Do you know what Mick said to me when he was walking onto the set? He said, 'With anyone else, I'd ask if they're ready to plug in, but Tess lives her whole life plugged in.' But honestly, the best part was the first day, sitting with them in the hotel suite. Just stripped down and themselves, in jeans, T-shirts, and reading glasses, sprawled out on the floor, talking and writing. No bullshit. Authentic. Here, I took some pics just for us to have," he said, sliding his phone across the table. "It was so beautiful."

Tess reached for Jack's hand.

"It was really special," he said.

"I thought the best part of the trip was when we were all done and the three of us went to that hole-in-the-wall Italian restaurant. We sat at the chef's table in the kitchen and Jack told us the most wonderful stories," she said, rubbing his hand. She turned back to the group. "Anyway, Mick and I were grateful to deliver messages we both hold dear."

"I appreciated what you said enormously," Luciana said. "I know it will inspire and motivate many other artists. You're changing the environment we work in for the better and showing what the arts mean in people's lives. Thank you."

Tess nodded in recognition.

"We came home too soon, though. *Time* is doing a cover story on Tess," Jack said.

"Please, don't remind me," she grumbled.

"I know, but baby, it's something to be proud of," he said, leaning forward and caressing her shoulders. "The title is 'Tess Lee Inspires the World, Dominates the Publishing Industry.' She refused to participate, so they're using stats and old quotes. I saw the preliminaries they sent over, and even I was speechless to revel in the totality of what she's done."

Tess turned to him and rolled her eyes.

"Okay, I see that's enough of that. I know I'll regret this, but how about another spin, my little salsa dancer?"

She smiled brightly. "Now you're talking." She turned to the group. "Luciana, are you and Joe ready for another whirl?"

"Actually, we have to head home. Joe has an early day tomorrow and I promised not to torture him for too long."

Joe laughed. "See you guys soon," he said. The two stood up, held hands, and said their goodnights.

"Bobby, stay for a while?" Jack said. "She won't make me dance as long if you're still here."

"Hey," Tess said, playfully hitting his chest.

"Sure. I'll have another," he said, downing the last of his beer.

Jack and Tess walked hand in hand to the dance floor. They danced to three songs, Tess smiling and laughing as Jack took her hand and twirled her around. With Jack's arm draped around her, they returned to the table, smiling and making googly eyes at each other like a pair of teenagers. They dropped in their seats and Jack guzzled his drink.

"She's really whipping me into shape," he said with a chuckle.

"Man, you two were on fire out there. Tess, where'd you learn to dance like that?" Suddenly, he paused, looked at Tess with a concerned expression, and said, "Tess, are you okay? Tess?"

She didn't respond.

Jack, noticing Bobby's face and tone change, said, "Tess?" With no response, he leapt up and flew over, kneeling in front of her chair. Her eyes were glazed over and she was mumbling. "Sweetheart, what's wrong? What is it?" he asked, taking her hands. She continued to mumble inaudibly. "Sweetheart, what's wrong?" he asked again. He leaned closer and put his ear to her mouth. "Jack, Jack," she was muttering, her whole body trembling.

"Sweetheart, I'm here. I'm listening." He touched her face, trying to bring her back to him.

"It can't be," she muttered. "He's supposed to be dead."

"Who, baby?"

She didn't say anything. He pulled slightly back, cupped her face in his hands, and looked directly in her eyes. "Sweetheart, who do you see?"

"My uncle. He just came in and sat at the bar. I thought he was dead. They told me he was dead."

"Are you sure it's him?"

She looked at him, terror in her eyes. "Jack, you know what he did to me," she said softly. "Do you think I could ever forget? He said… He said…"

He pulled her close, rubbing her back. "It's okay sweetheart, I'm here. I won't allow anything bad to happen to you." He leaned back and asked, "Where is he?"

"On the third stool, closest to us," she whispered.

Jack turned to look, rage sweeping across his face, his blood boiling. He took a breath and turned back to Tess. "What's his name?"

"Leonard. They called him Lenny," she whispered.

He pulled her close again, caressing the back of her head. He willed his voice to be calm and steady and he spoke softly into her ear. "I promise you're safe. No one will ever hurt you." He squeezed her hands and said, "Just wait a second." He rose and signaled for Bobby. They stepped away from the table and Jack asked, "Are you carrying?"

"Yeah, why?"

"Good. Take Tess home right now, don't let her out of your sight, and wait with her until I get there. Call Omar when you get in the car and ask him to meet you at our place."

"Jack, what the hell is going on?"

"Her uncle, the one who raped her for years, he's sitting at the bar."

"Holy shit. Jack, what are you going to do?"

"What needs to be done. Get Tess out of here and don't leave her side. Please."

Bobby nodded.

Jack knelt in front of Tess and said, "Sweetheart, Bobby is going to take you home. Please go with him. I'll be there soon."

"Jack," she said, looking at him, fear marring her delicate face.

He softly touched her cheek. "Sweetheart, please stand up and let Bobby get you out of here. I need you to go right now." He took her hand and helped her up.

"Come on, Tess, let's get you home," Bobby said, putting his arm around her and quickly ushering her out of the bar.

Jack sat down, a scowl on his face, his eyes glued to the man on the third stool. Half an hour later, Leonard got up. Jack followed him outside. He watched him get in a car, quickly got in his own, and followed him to a small, dilapidated house twenty minutes away. A moment after Leonard went inside and a light came on, Jack approached the house and knocked on the door. When the man answered, Jack said, "Are you Leonard?"

"Yes, who are you?" he replied.

Jack grabbed him by the neck, pushed him into a wall, and kicked the door closed behind them.

***

Jack walked into his house two hours later. Bobby and Omar were sitting in the living room.

"How's Tess?" he asked, taking a seat.

"She was shaken up, but she'll be all right," Omar said.

"Why aren't you with her?" Jack asked.

"Because she told us to wait out here for you. She was concerned about you. Don't worry, I've been checking on her. She fell asleep a little while ago. Was it really him?"

Jack nodded. "How did this happen? I thought he was dead."

Omar sighed. "About twelve or thirteen years ago, someone in her family reached out to her, said that her uncle had died. Her relatives are all liars. When Tess hit it big, none of them ever got a penny from her. She never wanted anything to do with them, for obvious reasons. Who knows, maybe they thought if he were out of the picture, Tess would reconnect with them and they'd hit the jackpot. It's the only thing I can think of."

"It doesn't matter. He'll never bother her again," Jack said.

"Did you kill him?" Bobby asked.

Jack shook his head. "But he'll be wishing he were dead for quite some time. It went against every instinct I have to let him live, but…"

"You were worried about Tess's reaction?" Omar said.

"I can't lie to her. I don't ever want to have to tell her I killed someone, even that bastard. I've killed dozens of people over the course of my career. Never wanted to, but I was able to do it, no problem. Tonight, I felt such intense anger and wanted him dead more than I can say, gutted by my own hands, but I couldn't do it."

"Is he in DC because of Tess? Did he follow you guys tonight?" Omar asked.

Jack shook his head. "It was a horrible coincidence. He didn't even see her there."

"How can you be sure?" Bobby asked.

"Believe me, he told me everything I wanted to know. He didn't hold anything back. Then I tortured him for sport, just so he'd remember me."

"Jack, what if he calls the police?" Omar asked.

"Trust me, he won't. He knows that I know what he's done. He doesn't want the police anywhere near him. He had some disturbing stuff in his place. And he had magazines with Tess on the cover."

"Fuck," Omar muttered.

"I should have killed him."

"Sounds like you nearly did," Omar said.

"Nearly, but he'll live. He's leaving DC. I made sure of that. He doesn't want me showing up at his door. Tess will never see him again. If he tries to hurt anyone else, he'll think of me. I told him I'd be watching, and I made him believe it."

"Tess is the sweetest person I know. I would have helped you if you'd asked," Bobby said. "Fuck, as a father, as a husband, I can't imagine how you felt."

"I've never felt so much hatred in my life. I thought I was going to explode. I didn't want to drag you further into it, and I needed you to bring Tess home. I should really go be with her. Can you guys let yourselves out?"

Omar nodded. "Jack, you should probably wash up before you see her. You have blood on you," he said, gesturing.

"Yeah," he mumbled, as he got up.

After cleaning up and changing clothes, he went to their bedroom, quietly opening the door. Tess jumped up. "Jack?"

"Yeah, baby," he said, rushing to her side. He sat on the edge of the bed and enfolded her in his arms. "I'm here, sweetheart."

She held him tightly and started crying.

"It's okay, sweetheart. I promise you'll never see him again."

She pulled back, sniffled, and he gently wiped her tears.

"Jack, where were you? What did you do?"

"It doesn't matter. I'm here now. Come on, lie down."

She lay down and Jack crawled into bed beside her. She rested her head on his chest and felt his steady breathing. He wrapped his arms around her and whispered, "Try to get some sleep, sweetheart. I'm right here with you and I'm not going anywhere." She closed her eyes, and soon they both fell asleep.

***

At five in the morning, Tess sprang up, screaming.

"It's okay, it's okay sweetheart," Jack said, trying to hold her.

Panting, she pulled away. He tried to hold her hand but she recoiled.

"Sweetheart, it's me. It's your Jack."

She looked at him, fear in her eyes.

"You had a nightmare," he said gently.

"It was awful. It was you and Lenny, your face and his, and…"

"Lenny is never going to hurt you again. It was just a bad dream."

"But where were you last night? What did you do? Why weren't you here with me?"

He reached his hand out again and she flinched.

"Sweetheart, please try to get some sleep. We can talk more about this in the morning. I don't want to upset you any more than you already are. It was a nightmare."

She looked at him differently than she had before, lay down on the far side of the bed away from him, and pulled the blanket up to her chin. Soon, she fell back into a restless sleep.

Troubled, Jack lay watching her until she woke up four hours later.

"Hi sweetheart," he said softly.

"Hi."

"How'd you sleep?"

"I had terrible dreams."

"Come here," he said, moving closer and opening his arms.

She avoided his arms and slipped out of bed. "I'm gonna take a shower," she mumbled on her way to the bathroom.

An hour later, Tess shuffled into the kitchen and sat on a barstool.

"I made breakfast," Jack said, handing her a mug of coffee. He ladled some oatmeal into a bowl and placed it in front of her.

"Jack, what happened last night?"

"Sweetheart, why don't we eat something first?"

"No," she said loudly, jumping to her feet. "Why won't you answer me? What have you done?"

He walked over and put his hand on her arm. "I'll tell you, but will you please sit down?"

She sat down and he took the stool next to her.

"I made sure he won't ever bother you again."

"Jack," she said softly, "did you kill him?" She looked down, as if terrified to hear the answer.

"No."

She looked him in the eyes. "Did you hurt him?"

"Tess…"

"Did you?"

"Yes."

"Oh my God," she muttered, turning her gaze down again.

He touched her arm and she flinched.

"How badly?" she asked.

"Tess…"

"How badly did you hurt him?"

"Enough that he'll always remember me."

"You tortured him?"

"Yes."

"Oh my God," she mumbled.

"Sweetheart," he said, reaching his hand out again.

She leapt up and started to walk away.

"Tess," he called.

"Please just leave me alone. I can't look at you."

***

Hours later, Jack went up to the office to find Tess sitting on the window seat, her legs outstretched. She didn't acknowledge him. He walked over and sat on the edge of the seat. He put his hand on her leg, but she pushed it away.

"Please, sweetheart, can you just look at me?"

"No. Please leave me alone."

"You haven't eaten anything all day. Can I at least bring you something?"

"I'm not hungry."

"Tess…"

She raised her gaze to meet his and flatly said, "I asked you to leave me alone."

He sat for a minute and then slowly stood up. "I know you're upset, but you have to talk to me sometime. And you need to eat something. Please come find me when you're ready." He went downstairs, collapsed onto the couch, and threw his head in his hands.

Five hours later, Tess meandered into the kitchen. She grabbed a bottle of water and was drinking it when Jack came over.

"Hey," he said softly.

When she didn't respond, he walked over and put his hand on her arm. She looked in his eyes.

"Sweetheart, please. We have to talk."

"What did you do to him?"

"Tess…"

She started to walk away.

He froze. "Please don't go."

"Then answer me. You said you wanted to talk, so talk. What did you do to him?"

"I taught him a lesson about pain."

Tess winced and dropped her head, speaking so softly he couldn't hear her. "Did you enjoy it?"

"What?"

"Tell me, Jack. Did you enjoy hurting him?" she said loudly.

"Yes. I did."

She huffed and shook her head. "Then you're no better than he is."

"How can you say that?"

"You know how I feel about violence. How could you do this?"

"I was protecting you."

"Vengeance isn't protection," she snapped.

"Tess, he's a pig. I should have killed him."

"I don't care about him; I care about you. The only darkness that frightens me is in you. I'm so angry at you. How could you do this to us, Jack?"

"He ruined your life, Tess!" he roared.

Tess gasped. Jack stepped forward, but she retreated and put her hand up.

"Tess…" he said softly.

She looked at him with something in her eyes he had never seen before. She took off her wedding band and locket, placed them on the counter, grabbed her handbag, and headed toward the front door.

"Tess, sweetheart, please. Where are you going?" he called.

"Do not follow me," she said quietly. She didn't look back.

Jack paced for hours. He texted Omar several times and learned he hadn't heard from Tess. When she hadn't returned home by eleven, he tracked her location using a discreet GPS program installed on her phone. She was at a bar several blocks away.

Jack entered the saloon and saw Tess sitting on a stool at the far end of the glossy, wooden bar, her shoulders slumped, a man sitting closely beside her. People at nearby tables were staring and taking pictures on their cell phones. Jack's blood started to simmer, but he tried to remain calm as he approached.

The man was talking to Tess. "There's a great bar a couple of blocks away if you want to have the next round somewhere else."

"She'll be leaving with me," Jack said forcefully, stepping between them.

"Jack," Tess said, looking up, her wide eyes whirling about as she slid on her stool, nearly falling over.

"Tess, sweetheart, let's get out of here," Jack said.

"Hey buddy, she's having a good time," the man said.

"Get the fuck out of here," Jack bellowed.

"Jack, you're being very rude to my new friend, Bill," Tess slurred, picking up her glass, the clear liquid sloshing about.

"Sweetheart…"

Tess pointed her finger at Jack and giggled. "Remember when *you* were my new friend I met in a bar? Hmm. It was a place just like this. Look how that turned out." She refocused her attention on her drink.

"Tess, do you know this guy?"

"Yeah, I'm her husband. Take a hike, Bill."

"Is he really your husband?" Bill asked Tess.

Tess just looked down.

"Looks to me like she doesn't want to see you. Maybe you should leave," Bill said.

Jack leaned in closer. "Let me say it again: she's my wife, and you're the one who is leaving. The only question is how many pieces you'll be in."

"Do you know how many guys have tried to talk to her tonight? I'm not going unless she asks me to, married or not."

"Listen asshole, take a long, hard look in my eyes. You do not want to mess with me."

Tess sighed. She turned to Bill and said, "You should probably go. He's always looking for a fight. He won't show you any mercy. He's good at hurting people. It's what he's trained for."

"Listen, if you're scared of him, I'll stay," Bill said. He put his hand on Tess's arm.

"Get your hand off of her," Jack seethed.

"It's okay. I'm not scared of him. Not like that, anyway," Tess mumbled.

Bill tossed some cash on the bar and stood up. Jack stayed close, forcing him to slither away.

When he was gone, Jack took his seat. "Tess, we need to talk."

She picked up her glass and threw back the last gulp. "Another," she said to the bartender. He grabbed the vodka bottle off the top shelf.

Jack put his hand up, "She's had enough."

"I'm not a child and I'm not driving. I'll have another, please," she said to the bartender.

"She doesn't drink," Jack said.

"Is she an alcoholic?" the bartender asked.

"I most certainly am not," Tess slurred.

Jack shook his head. "No, she just doesn't drink."

"She hasn't been overserved. It's her choice, buddy," the bartender replied as he filled her glass.

Tess grabbed her drink and started downing it.

"Please, Tess, let me take you home," Jack said.

She put her glass down, furrowed her brow, turned to him, and asked, "How did you know where to find me?"

"I installed a program on your phone."

"*What*?" she asked angrily. "You spy on me?"

"It was after Ray stalked you and I read all of that weird fan mail you get. I only did it as a precaution. I've never looked at it before tonight. You have my word."

"Your word?" she said, letting out a huff. "For what that's worth." She took another sip of her drink.

"Sweetheart, please. I'm so sorry about earlier, about everything. Let's get out of here, get something in your stomach, and we can talk."

"I'm not going anywhere with you. Leave."

"I will not leave you here."

"Jack, I'm not going home with you. Just go."

"If you don't want to come home with me, that's fine. Tell me where you want to go and I'll take you, but there's no way I'm leaving you here."

"I don't believe you."

"If you want to go to a friend's house or a hotel, I'll drive you. I won't leave you here."

She picked up her drink, guzzled the rest of it, and placed the empty glass on the bar. "Fine, you can take me to Omar and Clay's." She opened her bag to get money to pay the bill, but Jack took a fifty out of his pocket and threw it down.

"Come on, sweetheart. Let's go."

She tripped as she stood, unsteady on her feet. Jack offered his hand, but she hissed, "Don't touch me," and tottered ahead of him. When they got in the car, she said, "I'm going to call Omar."

"Tess, please come home. We've never spent a night apart. You can just get some sleep if you want. We can talk tomorrow."

"You said you'd take me anywhere I want to go," she said. She put her hand on the door handle. "I'm getting out."

He locked the doors. "Fine, call Omar."

When they arrived at the apartment building, Omar and Clay were waiting outside. Jack unlocked the doors and Tess turned to open hers. He put his hand on her arm. "Hey, please just wait one minute."

She turned to look at him, her eyes glazed with sadness.

"Tess, I love you with my whole heart, forever. I'm so sorry. Get some sleep and I'll come pick you up tomorrow."

"Jack, please just leave me alone. That's all I want." With that, she opened the door and stumbled out of the car.

"Hi, Butterfly," Omar said. "Come on. Clay will help you up and I'll be there in a jiff."

Clay put his arm around Tess and guided her into their building.

Jack opened the passenger side window and leaned over to talk to Omar. "She had a lot to drink and she hasn't eaten anything today."

"We'll try to get something in her. Are you okay?"

"No, I'm not. I can't believe this is happening."

"She's just upset. I'm sure she'll see things more clearly after some rest."

"Please take good care of her," Jack said.

"Of course."

"If she changes her mind and wants to come home, call me and I'll be right over."

Omar nodded solemnly.

"I'll call tomorrow."

Omar went up to his apartment and Jack drove away.

CHAPTER 8

After taking four ibuprofen and eating a small banana at Omar's insistence, Tess slipped into a borrowed T-shirt and pair of boxer shorts and passed out in the guest room. Three hours later, she woke up screaming. Omar and Clay flew into the room and switched on a light.

"Butterfly, you're okay. Clay and I are here," Omar said, sitting on the side of the bed. She reached out for him and he wrapped his arms around her. "It was just a bad dream," he said softly, rubbing the back of her head. She started to cry.

"It was awful," she gasped between sobs. "Lenny and Jack, and I was trying to get away, but they were too strong, and..."

"Shh... it was just a bad dream. You're okay. Jack would never hurt you."

She pulled back and wiped her eyes. Clay handed her a box of tissues. "Thank you," she muttered.

"Butterfly, would you like me to stay in here with you tonight?"

She shook her head. "I'm okay. You two should go back to sleep. I'm sorry for being such a bother."

"Nonsense," Clay said. "We're here for anything you need."

"Always and forever," Omar said, embracing her again.

"I'm okay," she sniveled.

"Please holler if you need us," Omar said, switching off the light.

Tess soon fell back to sleep. Two hours later, she awoke from another violent nightmare, although this time she was quiet and didn't disturb anyone. Afraid to sleep, she wandered into the living room and turned the television on quietly. She flipped through the stations, bypassing a plethora of infomercials, and landed on a special about supernovas on PBS. She grabbed a throw blanket, curled up, and watched.

***

"Good morning, Butterfly. Smells like a bakery in here; what have you been up to?" Omar asked, walking over and pecking the top of her head.

"I couldn't sleep so I made you guys pancakes. I covered them with foil to keep them warm."

"That was so sweet," Clay said, tearing the foil off the plate.

"I used cinnamon and vanilla for you, Clay."

"You know they're my favorite. Thank you."

"Butterfly, you must be starving. Can I fix you a plate?"

"I'm not hungry, but coffee would be great."

"I'm on it," Clay said.

Omar sighed. "You would feel better if you ate something."

"Please don't," she said.

"You know Jack has already texted me twice this morning to check on you. He's worried."

"He's left me half a dozen voicemails. I don't want to talk to him."

"Butterfly, he loves you. Don't you think…"

"Please just stop. I don't want to talk to him. I don't want to see him. My God, do you realize what he did? He tortured someone, Omar. He *tortured* him. And he enjoyed it. I asked him and he admitted it. He hurts people. He's… he's violent," she said, her eyes welling.

"Frankly, I'm surprised he didn't kill him. If I had been there, I would have," Omar said.

"No you wouldn't have," Tess said.

"I absolutely would have."

"I doubt that," Clay said.

"That asshole? You can bloody well bank on it. I would have relished the chance. I'm not a violent man, but I wouldn't have thought twice about it. Butterfly, can you really blame Jack? He was defending you against an animal."

"Omar, he has a history of violence. He was trained to torture and kill people, and now I'm afraid that…"

"That was for his work. You've always understood that in the past. He would never hurt someone innocent," Omar replied.

"You always do this; you always take his side and you don't listen to me."

"Butterfly…"

"I mean it," she said, staring straight into his eyes, tears in her own. "Like with the prenup. I can't believe you did that behind my back."

Omar inhaled deeply. "I knew that would come up at some point."

"Well of course. How do you think that made me feel?"

"He was just trying to do the honorable thing. I thought it showed a lot of integrity."

"It isn't about what you thought. That's the point. You don't respect me."

"Butterfly…"

Clay interrupted. "Tess is right. Why don't you listen to her?"

"You too?" Omar said.

"I'm just being honest. Tess has a right to be upset with you. And she has a right to feel however she chooses about her husband. I know you love her, but she's entitled to have her feelings. Do you remember how Raj accused you of infantilizing her? Perhaps you should consider that he might have had a point."

Tess stood up and opened her handbag. She retrieved a pack of cigarettes and a book of matches. "I'm going outside for some air," she said.

Ten minutes later, she was sitting on the stoop puffing away on her second cigarette when Omar came outside. "May I join you?" he asked.

She shrugged.

He sat down beside her. "When did you start smoking again?"

"I bought a pack last night. Don't give me a hard time."

"I won't." They sat in silence for a couple of minutes. Eventually, Omar said, "Tess, you're right and I'm sorry. I know you're going through a dreadful time right now and I'll support you anyway you choose. I do respect you beyond measure. I only want to help. All I know is how much you love Jack and how happy he makes you."

Tess took a drag on her cigarette and stomped it out. "I don't know if I can ever be with him again after what he did. I've never felt so lost and heartbroken in my life, not for a moment, nothing like this pain."

"Butterfly, I'm so sorry," he said, rubbing her back.

"When I couldn't sleep last night, I watched something on TV about supernovas, which is basically when massive stars explode.

They say a supernova is so luminous that it's like an entire galaxy, but then there's nothing, just a black hole. Maybe that's like me and Jack. I always felt like we burned so brightly, but maybe now after this explosion, there won't be anything left to salvage. We just won't exist anymore."

"You know, I saw part of that special too." He leaned back on his hands and looked up at the sky. "What I remember is that the shock wave created by a supernova can cause the formation of new stars. Maybe that's what it will be like for you and Jack. Yes, you're going through something hugely dark right now, but maybe from this experience you'll create new light."

"Can I tell you something? Will you promise not to repeat it?" she asked.

"Of course."

"He said that he did it because Lenny ruined my life." She burst into tears. After taking a moment to compose herself, she looked at Omar and said, "That's what he thinks. He thinks my life was ruined."

Omar sighed. "Oh, Butterfly. I know how Jack feels about you, how truly he loves you. I can't imagine he meant it that way. It must have been something that slipped out in the heat of the moment. He was thinking about your childhood, not your life."

"I don't know. All I know is that everything hurts right now."

"You know I'll do anything for you; Clay will, too. What can I do to help?"

"I need some time and space. I just want to stay here for a while. Will you please stop by my place and pick up some things for me?"

He nodded. "I'll call Jack and let him know to expect me."

***

"Hey," Jack said, letting Omar in.

"How are you holding up?" Omar asked.

"Not well. How's Tess?"

"Why don't we go take a seat in the living room?" Omar suggested.

"Can I get you something?"

Omar shook his head. "I'm fine, thanks."

Jack sat on the couch and Omar took the adjacent chair. "How's Tess?" Jack asked again.

"Not good. She's having nightmares. Not eating. She's devastated."

"What's she saying?"

"Jack, this is so hard for me because I truly love you both. Tess is quite angry at me, and as I've realized, rightfully so. In my desire to look out for her, I haven't always given her the credit she deserves. I won't make that mistake again. She'll share with you if she wants to, but I won't violate her privacy and trust by telling you anything she's said in confidence. I hope you can understand that."

"Yeah, okay," Jack muttered. "I only wanted to defend her, to protect her. You know what that son of a bitch did to her." He looked down and shook his head. "Now the things Tess has said, the way she looks at me, it's as if... it's as if she thinks I'm like him."

"Jack, there's something we've never spoken about, something I thought about when I was attacked. Perhaps it will help you understand."

"Please tell me."

"I suspect you spent most of your career with the Bureau going after people who look like me. I mean, that's what counterterrorism was all about at that time. Is that true?" Omar asked.

Jack nodded.

"I can only assume that you've racially profiled people, even though the party line is of course that such a thing never happens."

"Yes."

"You spent years, shall we say, forcefully interrogating people who look like me. I'm sure most were evil to the core, but no one bats a hundred. I can only assume there were those who were innocent."

Jack looked down.

"I'm not angry with you in any way. I understand the impossible job you had. Truthfully, I have no doubt that the net gain of your actions has made the world safer. But for people who look like me, there's also been a very steep price to pay. You've been part of the system that created the men who attacked me."

"Omar…"

"You don't need to say anything. I understand that the world we live in is complex with many shades of gray. We share that in common. But Tess… she sees only black and white."

"Yeah, I know," Jack said.

"You and I have had to see shades of gray to survive the worlds in which we live. Tess has had to see black and white, dark and light, in order to survive hers. It's not that either is necessarily right or better, but they are different. Violence is violence to Tess. That's why what you did is so hard for her. Your motivation is irrelevant; only the action matters."

Jack took a deep breath and exhaled slowly. "It's funny because one of the things that attracted me to her from the first night we met was the way she sees the world, her ability to focus on light. I just wanted to be near her good, compassionate energy. I had hoped it would rub off on me."

Omar smiled faintly. "I understand. I saw the same thing in her from the moment we met. And it has changed you, Jack, just as it has changed me. You're a different man. I've seen the darkness in you dwindle over these last few years. You're lighter."

"Do you think she's afraid of me?"

"I think she's afraid that you're capable of hurting people. You have a history because of your years as an agent. I think she's afraid that what you did to Lenny isn't an aberration. And I think she's afraid that if she condones what you did to him, it's no different than condoning what he did to her. It's a moral quagmire for someone like her."

"Was I wrong, Omar? I know I was blinded by rage, but what would you have done if you had been there that night?" Jack asked.

"It's not my place to make moral judgments, but as I told Tess, I would have killed him. If I had been there that night, if I had the opportunity and could get away with it, I absolutely would have killed him with my bare hands, sure as I'm sitting here. She doesn't believe that's true, nor does Clay, but I'm telling you, I would have been capable of it. But there are two important differences."

"What?"

"Well, I don't have a history of aggression. I've never harmed anyone in my life. And then there's the most important difference."

"Which is?"

"Tess and I don't have the same kind of relationship you two have. We don't have sex."

Jack looked down.

"Although I don't practice, I am a trained psychologist. Examining this situation from that perspective, I suspect it's confusing for her—the man she loves, the man she's intimate with, brutalizing the man that repeatedly raped her. There's a troubling mixture of violence and sex, involving the man who hurt her most and the one whom she loves and trusts the most. I believe that what you did to Lenny muddled it in her mind. Now she has to work through it. I'm not going to push her, and I'm not sure that you should either. She needs time."

"Omar, I love Tess with all my heart. She's everything to me. Our marriage is everything to me. Please, you have to help us."

"I believe you and Tess belong together, Jack, and I've told her as much. But right now, I need to help Tess in whatever way *she* wants."

"Last night was the only night we've ever spent away from each other. Since the night we met, we've never slept apart. It was hell for me." Jack dropped his head and softly said, "I know her. It's hell for her, too. We can't fix this if we're not under the same roof. Please, you have to convince her to come home so we can work it out."

"I hope she chooses to come back here because I do believe that's what will ultimately bring her the most happiness. But right now, I'm going to give Tess whatever she wants, including a safe place to stay. I need to be there for her in whatever way she decides. I'll tell her what I think insofar as she wants to hear it, but I'm not going to impose anything on her or manipulate her feelings. I hope you can understand."

"Yeah, I do," he mumbled reluctantly. "Will you please tell her that I said I love her and I want her to come home?"

"Of course."

"And Omar, please take good care of her."

"I promise."

"I packed some of her things. I'll go get the bag," Jack said, rising.

"Jack…"

"Yeah?" he asked, turning.

"If it helps at all, I know how much you love each other. I truly believe you belong together, and I just know you'll find your way back to each other."

"Thanks," Jack muttered. "I'll be right back."

***

When Omar got home, he didn't see Tess. He knocked on the guest room door.

"Come in," she said, propping herself up in bed.

"Hi, Butterfly," he said, putting her bag down and sitting beside her.

"Thank you for getting my things."

"Sure. Whatever you need. Jack asked me to tell you how much he loves you and that he hopes you'll come home. He looked like an absolute wreck."

She turned her gaze downward and shook her head. "I can't. I can't face him yet."

Omar put his hand on hers. "I know. Take all the time you need. You're welcome to stay here as long as you like. Clay and I love having you. Hell, I think you're the roommate Clay always wanted, which is making me look bad," he said with a little laugh.

Tess smiled.

"How about something to eat? You must be famished."

"I'm not really hungry," she said.

"Maybe you can just pick a little. Butterfly, please try. It will be harder to sort through things if you're feeling weak. We can watch a movie. How about our old standby, *Moulin Rouge*?"

"A love story? Really, Omar?"

"Sorry, wasn't thinking. I'm guessing slasher films are out too. Hmm, what can we watch without romance or violence?"

"I'd settle for something without men."

"Lesbian porn it is. Shall I make popcorn?"

Tess giggled.

"It's good to see you smile, Butterfly, even for a moment. Come on, let's watch a movie. Your choice."

"Anything I want?"

"Yes, Butterfly, *anything*."

"Even *Beaches*?"

He rolled his eyes dramatically. "Bloody hell, even *Beaches*. If you behave, I may even serenade you. You know you're the wind beneath my wings."

She smiled. "I'm going to unpack first. I'll be out in a few minutes."

He kissed her forehead and left.

Tess grabbed her bag and placed it on the bed. She unzipped it and immediately saw a jewelry box atop a notecard. She opened the box to reveal her heart locket. The card read: "I love you with my whole heart, forever. Please come home. Jack." She shut her eyes, held the locket tightly in her hands, and inhaled deeply.

"Butterfly, how about I make grilled cheese? You can nibble," Omar hollered.

"Okay," she called. "On my way," she said, sticking the necklace in her pocket.

***

That night, Tess woke up at two o'clock in the morning, screaming "no," at the top of her lungs. Omar and Clay raced into the room. They both sat on the bed. Omar gently held her in his arms.

"It's okay, Butterfly. You're okay," he whispered, rubbing her back. After a few minutes, he asked, "Do you want me to stay in here with you?"

She nodded.

Two hours later, she awoke like a bolt again, screaming and gasping for breath. Omar comforted her. Eventually, they fell back asleep.

Tess finally woke up just after ten.

"Good morning, Butterfly."

She turned to see him seated beside her on the bed, leaning against pillows.

"Morning. How long have you been awake?"

"A little while. Glad you got some rest. Come here," he said, holding his arms open.

She moved closer and burrowed into his chest. "Thank you for staying with me," she whispered.

"Of course. It kind of reminded me of all those nights we spent curled up in your college dorm on that twin bed with the awful mattress. Remember those days?"

"How could I forget? Any time we were holiday orphans, or some asshole broke your heart, or when I got a bad grade or a writing rejection, we'd just snuggle together until everything felt better."

He kissed the top of her head. "I wish it were that easy now."

"Me too."

"Tess, for fear of being thrown out of the bed, I have to ask: isn't Jack the one you really want to be with like this?"

"I miss him so much I don't even have words for it. And the thought of it being like this forever, of us not being together, hurts more than anything I've ever felt."

"Then why not go to him and try to work it out?"

"I've always thought of Jack as the most gentle, loving man I've ever known. When I replay every minute we've spent together, that's what I remember. I've always seen him a certain way, and I thought he saw me a certain way. Everything we share is based on how we see each other. Has been since the night we met. And now, after what he did, I don't know if I trust that anymore." She paused and looked into Omar's eyes. "What if it's all wrong? What if he isn't who I think he is?"

"Oh, Butterfly, I'm not saying what Jack did was right, but it's understandable. Even if it isn't to you, even if that act stands outside of time, it doesn't change all the other moments you've shared. You said yourself that he's never been anything but gentle and loving, every day for years. He's a good man, but he's not perfect. Perhaps things aren't always as black and white as we would like them to be. He is gentle and loving, *and* he did this terrible thing. He is both. He is a shade of gray, light and dark together. Perhaps even good men are capable of doing harm. The question is, can you forgive him?"

She slung her arm across his waist. "I don't know yet."

"Come on, how about we get some breakfast? You've hardly eaten a thing in days. Let's make an omelet and curl up on the couch and watch movies. Clay's at work so we have the place to ourselves."

"Okay," she said.

"Good," he said, standing up. "In the tone of *Beaches*, retch retch, I vote for movies that celebrate friendship because I don't know how I'd survive without you."

She smiled.

He reached his hand out, she latched onto it, and they rolled out of bed.

***

At eight o'clock that night, Tess, Omar, and Clay were finishing dinner. Tess was laughing at a story Clay was telling when her phone rang. She looked to see that it was Jack. Again.

"Butterfly, he's been calling all day. He really did look like a wreck yesterday."

She took a deep breath and answered.

"Hey," she said.

"Hey."

"Just give me a minute so I can have some privacy," she said. Omar squeezed her hand in support and they looked at each other. She let go and took her phone into the guest room, climbing into bed.

"Hey, I'm here," she said.

"Thank you for answering. How are you doing, sweetheart?"

"This is awful. I'm terrible."

"Me too, baby. Please, I'm begging you, come home. It's the only way things will get better."

"Jack, I need time to sort through my feelings."

"About me? I'm your husband and I love you with all my heart. You know me."

"It isn't that simple anymore. Not after the things you've said and done."

"Tess, I'm only a man. I know I've made mistakes. Please try to remember all the good things we've shared. Since the day we met, I've tried to put you first above everything else. Our marriage has been my top priority. I'm completely committed to you. Anytime you've needed me, I've been there. There's not a day that's gone by when I haven't tried to tell and show you how much you mean to me. I've been there through all the hard times. I held you when your father contacted you and you sank into that dark depression. I bathed and dressed you after the car accident. Tess, sweetheart, I'm still that same man." He paused before continuing, "I've never asked for anything but your love, but I'm asking now. Please come home."

"I'm not ready to talk about what you did to Lenny. I need time and space to figure out how I feel and why I feel that way. I don't want to be pressured."

"You won't be. I give you my word that if you come home, I'll keep my distance. I'll give you as much time and space as you need, no matter how long it takes. I'll follow your lead. Please baby, please just come home. I need you. I know in my heart this won't get better until we're in one place together. Please, Tess."

"Jack, if I do this, you have to be true to your word. I'm dealing with a lot and I need to work through it my own way."

"I promise."

"Okay," she said softly.

"I'll come get you."

"No, that's okay. I'll have Omar drop me off."

"I'll be waiting for you."

CHAPTER 9

Jack was waiting in the kitchen when Tess walked into their home. She put her bag down.

"Hey," he said.

"Hey."

"Thank you for coming home."

"Jack, I remember every minute of our relationship. I remember everything you've ever done for me—pulling me out of my depression when my father died, helping me shower and watching me sleep after the car accident—and everything else you've done every single day since we met. That's why this is all so incredibly painful. You don't need to remind me. It's not like I could ever forget."

"I know. I'm sorry; I didn't mean it like that. I just desperately wanted you to come home. Spending two nights without you killed me. I needed you here so we can work it out."

"Jack, you promised if I came home, you'd give me space and time. Please, that's what I need. I'm not ready."

"Like I said on the phone, you can have all the space you need. I won't pressure you. I'm just glad you're here."

"I'm tired. I'm going to sleep."

"There's just one thing I have to say to you."

"What?"

"Tess, I love you so much. I need you to know that."

"Jack, I do know that. I love you too, more than anything. Love isn't the issue."

"Then what is it?"

"Trust. I love you, but I don't know if I can be with you anymore."

They stood, just looking at each other, the air between them heavy. After a moment passed, Jack picked up Tess's bag and quietly said, "I'll bring this to our room for you."

***

At one in the morning, Tess woke up screaming.

Jack sprang up and tried to put his hand on her. She flung his arm away and jumped out of bed, panting and mumbling, "They're dying. They're dying." She raced out of the room and up to the office, Jack following behind.

She ran to the bookshelf where she kept all her novels and started pulling them off the shelf, each one making a thud as it hit the floor. Jack stood in the doorway, helpless. "Sweetheart, what are you doing?"

Tess sat on the floor in a heap of her books, picking them up and frantically flipping through the pages before tossing each one back to the ground. "They're dying," she repeated.

Jack stepped forward but Tess put her hand out and said, "Don't. Don't come near me."

He stopped in his tracks. "Tess, you had a nightmare. Please, tell me what's going on."

She started weeping, her head hung, tears trickling onto her scattered books. Eventually she looked up. Her cries slowed and she quietly said, "They're dying. All my characters are dying. I never imagine what happens to them after the last page, but now they're all dying, one by one. I'm watching their burials."

"Tess, please sweetheart, let me come over and help you."

"Don't come near me. You did this," she whimpered. "You did this. I had two things. I had you and I had writing. Now you've taken them both."

"Sweetheart, I'm so sorry. Please let me help you," he said, taking a small step forward.

"No!" she screamed, grabbing a framed wedding photo from a nearby table and throwing it across the room.

He dodged it, his eyes and mouth wide open in shock as the frame smashed into the wall and glass shattered everywhere.

Tess started weeping again. She looked up at him. "Now I have nothing. You've taken everything from me, even myself."

"Tess…"

"Go. Just go," she said softly, her cheeks wet and salty.

He stood and stared at her for a moment, her books strewn on the floor, glass around his feet. He stepped out of the room and shut the door. Stunned, he leaned against the wall, threw his head in his hands, and tried to catch his breath as his eyes stung with the rush of hot tears. Suddenly, he heard Tess scream. He flung the office door open and saw her in the pile of broken glass, her hand bleeding. He flew over and scooped her up.

"Jack, it's okay. I was just trying to clean it up and I cut my hand," she said softly.

He carried her over the broken shards and all the way down to their bathroom.

"Jack, you're overreacting. I'm fine."

When they got to their bathroom, he put her down in front of the sink, turned the faucet on cold, and held her hand under the flowing water. After a couple of minutes, he switched the faucet off, flipped the toilet seat cover down, and said, "Please sit."

She sat down.

"Let me see it," he said gently.

She held the palm of her hand open and he examined the cut.

"I'm fine," she muttered.

He scoured the bathroom cabinet for hydrogen peroxide and poured some onto a cotton ball. "This will sting a little," he said quietly, as he held it to her wound. She winced. After a few seconds he removed the cotton ball, knelt on the floor before her, and started gently blowing on the cut. She watched his lips form a circle as he softly blew soothing air onto the wound. She put her hand on his temple and tenderly brushed the side of his face. Their eyes met. After a moment passed, he stood up, got a bandage, and placed it over her cut. He turned to leave the room.

"Jack," she called.

He stopped in the doorway and looked back at her.

"Thank you."

"Yeah," he muttered. "I'm going to clean up the glass. You should try to go back to sleep."

"Jack," she called again.

"Yeah."

"There's something I didn't say earlier tonight that I should have."

His eyes were fixed to hers.

"When I said I don't know if I can be with you anymore, I should have said that I want to. I desperately want to be with you more than anything."

He smiled faintly. "Go back to bed, sweetheart. I'll be down soon."

CHAPTER 10

The next morning, Tess woke up on the far edge of the bed, her back to Jack. She lay still for a few minutes and eventually craned her neck to see if he was still asleep. He lay facing her on the other side of the bed, wide awake. Without uttering a word, she turned back around, slid out of bed, and wandered to the bathroom. She emerged ten minutes later in running clothes. Jack was sitting on the edge of the bed, his head down and shoulders slumped.

"You going for a run?" he asked, looking up.

She nodded and left without a word. An hour later, she returned, dripping with sweat. Jack was in the kitchen reading the newspaper. He glanced up and smiled awkwardly at her.

"I'm gonna take a shower," she said, barely looking at him.

Half an hour later, she emerged, freshly showered and dressed.

"I made more coffee," Jack said.

"Thanks," she mumbled, pouring herself a mug. Jack watched as she opened the cabinets and surveyed the food before shutting them without taking anything. She grabbed her coffee and headed up to the office.

In the middle of the afternoon, Tess returned to the kitchen. Jack sat at the counter, eating a sandwich and reviewing a file for a consulting job.

"Hey," he said. "Can I get you something?"

"I'm fine, thanks," she said.

He observed as she took a tub of almonds, spilled some onto the counter, methodically counted two piles of twelve, and put the rest back. She grabbed two napkins and scooped up each pile of nuts, stacked them in her hand, grabbed a water bottle, and went back upstairs.

Three hours later, Jack ventured up to the office. Tess was seated on the window seat, her legs extended, smoking a cigarette out the open window. There was an ashtray beside her with several extinguished butts. He stood in the doorway, watching his wife and feeling a million miles away from her. She glanced over at him, palpable sadness in her eyes.

"Hey," he said. "I was thinking about getting something delivered for dinner. What do you feel like?"

"Nothing, I'm fine," she said, returning her gaze to the window.

"Tess, I know you want me to leave you alone, but please, you need to eat something." Moments passed without a response, so he said, "How about I order Thai food? You can just pick a little if you feel like it."

She shrugged apathetically. "Whatever you want."

Two hours later, she came downstairs and found Jack watching television in the living room, Thai containers spread out on the coffee table.

"There's plenty of food left. It's all vegetarian," he said.

She sat down and he handed her a plate. She scanned the food and, after some consideration, selected a summer roll. Instead of biting into it, she started pulling it apart, taking out small morsels of food. She took a piece of shaved carrot, followed by a bean sprout, which she popped in her mouth, one at a time. Eventually, she had eaten the contents of the summer roll, bit by bit, leaving the wrapping on her plate.

"I'm tired. I'm going to bed," she said softly. "I'll help you clean up."

"That's okay. I've got it," he said.

"Goodnight then," she said, heading to their bedroom.

At three in morning, Tess sprang up from a violent nightmare, screaming and shaking. She was rocking back and forth, her breathing quick and shallow.

Jack scooched closer and gently said, "Please Tess, let me comfort you."

Tears started falling from her eyes.

"Please sweetheart," he said again. "Just let me comfort you. I don't expect anything in return."

She nodded and he threw his arms around her, pulling her trembling body close to him. "It's okay, sweetheart. It's okay. I've got you," he said softly.

"Make them stop," she whimpered.

"You're okay. It's just a bad dream. No one's ever going to hurt you again. I won't allow it."

"He said no one will ever love me," she whispered.

"I love you, Tess. I love you so much. I love you so much," he said gently, cradling her in his arms, his cheek firm against hers.

She rested her head on his shoulder and he held her in his embrace, continuing to whisper, "It's okay. It's okay. I love you. I love you so much, with my whole heart."

When she calmed down, he said, "Here, let's lie down, sweetheart," guiding her head onto the pillow. He curled up right behind her, draped his arm over her, and asked, "Is this okay?"

She put her hand on his arm and pushed her body closer to his. Soon they fell back asleep.

When Tess woke up the next morning, Jack was still holding her. She studied his hand, hovering her fingers just millimeters from his skin. When she could no longer resist the urge, she gingerly touched the tips of her fingers to the tips of his.

"Hey, good morning," he said.

"Good morning," she muttered, quickly slipping out of bed. She sprinted into the bathroom, returning ten minutes later in running clothes. Just like that, she was out the door.

Jack watched in agony as she again drank only coffee for breakfast. At lunchtime, she meandered downstairs. Jack leapt up. "Hi! How about I fix us something to eat?"

"I'm okay, thanks," she said, grabbing an apple from the fruit bowl. Pink lady in hand, she turned to leave but then shimmied back around and looked at Jack. They stared at each other. She opened her mouth, but a moment passed without any words spoken. She turned around and headed upstairs, munching on her apple.

At six o'clock, she came downstairs again. Jack was sitting at the counter in the kitchen, working on his laptop. "Hey," he said, looking up.

"Jack," she said softly. Before she could continue, his phone rang.

He glanced down. "It's Bobby. I can let it go to voicemail."

"No, you should answer it."

"Yeah, okay." He swiped to answer. "Hey, Bobby. What's up? … I'm staying in with Tess tonight."

"Jack…" Tess said.

"Hang on, Bobby," Jack said, blocking the microphone with his hand. He looked at Tess. "Yeah?"

"What does Bobby want?" she asked.

"He and Joe invited me out for a drink."

"Oh, well, you should go," she said.

"Tess, I don't need to go. I want to stay with you."

"You've been cooped up here for days. It's not healthy. Go out. See your friends."

"I don't want to leave you."

"Go, Jack. Really, I'm fine."

He looked at her longingly, then picked up the phone and said, "I'll see you guys in half an hour."

CHAPTER 11

Joe and Bobby were already seated at a table when Jack arrived at Shelby's. They had a beer waiting for him.

"We figured you could use this," Bobby said, sliding the bottle over.

"Thanks," he replied, taking a swig.

"You look like crap," Bobby said.

"Yeah, I feel like crap."

"Well, Tess moved back home when you asked her to. That's a good sign," Bobby said.

"When she came home, I told her how much I love her. She told me she loves me too. Then she said love isn't the issue, trust is, and that she doesn't know if she can be with me anymore. Tess never says anything she doesn't mean. I'm terrified she might leave me over this."

"I don't know if this helps at all, but I would have done the same thing in your position. If someone hurt Gina or Rob like that, I'm telling you, I'd have killed him, no question. I think you showed restraint," Bobby said.

"Omar said the same thing, that he'd have killed him too, and he meant it. But all that matters to Tess is what I did. I was blinded by rage and I made a choice. Now I have to live with it."

"This all must be very traumatic for Tess. How's she doing?" Joe asked.

"She's having nightmares. Her eating disorder is back. She looks sad all the time. Beyond that, I don't know."

"What do you mean you don't know?" Joe asked.

"She's not visibly angry at me anymore, but we're living in virtual silence. It's brutal."

"You two love each other like you're in a movie or something. You'll work it out," Bobby said.

"Absolutely," Joe said.

"I don't know. When I convinced her to come back home, I promised to give her space, but it's so hard. I feel like I should be doing something to fix this. Every hour that goes by feels like an eternity. It just feels worse and worse. I don't know how it'll ever get better if we stay like this."

"Fight for her," Bobby said. "Hang out with us to clear your head, and then you go home and fight for her."

"I'm afraid she'll leave again, and that if she does, she may never come back. I don't want to force her. I promised not to pressure her. I didn't know how hard it would be, walking around the house like a couple of shadows passing each other. Last night she was crying and I begged her to let me hold her, just to comfort her. I can't tell you how good it felt to put my arms around her. But then today…"

"What?" Joe asked.

"We were two shadows again. There were moments when I thought maybe she wanted something from me, but I wasn't sure, so I kept my distance."

"You have to find out. Show her you're in this thing for the long haul," Bobby said.

Jack took a swill from his beer. He looked at Joe and asked, "What do you think?"

"Jack, you know Tess better than anyone else, so you have to feel this out. If she asked for space, maybe you should respect that. From what I know of the situation, it seems that respecting her wishes is a part of this whole thing. Maybe there's a way to reach out to her without it feeling like you're asking for too much."

"Maybe. Enough about me. What's going on with you guys?"

"Well, it's not as bad as what you're going through, but we're all having women problems," Joe said.

"What's up with you and Luciana?"

"I asked her to move in with me. She said no."

"Oh Joe, I'm so sorry. Did she say why?"

"She likes things the way they are. She wants to stay together, exclusively, but she wants us each to have our own place. Her logic is, 'If it ain't broke, don't fix it.' She's also worried that our schedules won't gel if we live together. You know my work schedule is pretty regimented. But Luciana's an artist; she works when inspiration strikes, sometimes through the night and then she sleeps during the day, or sometimes she'll spend days on end sculpting. She doesn't want to be constrained by having to consider someone she's living with."

"And you?" Jack asked.

"I honestly don't know. Part of me thinks she's right. Things have been wonderful. But then I think about having someone to wake up with every morning and fall asleep with every night. Part of me desperately wants that, and I want it with her. I'm almost sixty and I've lived alone my entire adult life. I'm ready for a constant companion."

Jack rolled the beer bottle in his hand. "The happiest moments of my entire life have been the simple things since I met Tess: falling asleep and waking up together, or coming through the door and seeing her smile at me, or when I'm making coffee and she walks in the room and touches my arm. Just having her there."

"You and Tess will work things out. Everyone knows you belong together. Deep down, Tess knows that too," Joe said.

"I'm sorry. We were talking about you and Luciana. I know what she means about the artist thing. When Tess is really immersed in a new novel, she'll often work for more than twelve hours in a row. Sometimes we'll sleep on the sofa in the office, so she can get up whenever she wants to write."

"And it never bothers you? Did it interfere with your schedule when you were working full time at the Bureau?"

Jack shook his head. "Tess and I never tried to change each other. I'm not creative like she is, and I love seeing her work. I love seeing her passion, not just for me, but for art. It's hard to explain. It never interfered with anything. I've always seen it more like a gift, a glimpse into a world I wouldn't otherwise get to see, a world that's beautiful and hopeful and full of light. The world we've fought to protect."

"Maybe it could be like that for you and Luciana, too," Bobby said. "You should tell her that you won't try to change her, that you just want to be with her. Fight for her."

"That seems to be your advice to everyone tonight. What's going on with you and Gina?" Joe asked.

Bobby sighed. "Dude, we haven't had sex in months. I'm going crazy."

"Well, you two have a baby. She's exhausted," Joe said.

"Plus her body's probably changed since giving birth. Maybe she's self-conscious," Jack said.

Bobby took a swig of his beer. "I think it's more than that. Since we got married, we haven't been doing it that much, other than when we were trying to get pregnant. She doesn't seem interested. Is that normal?"

"Every couple is different," Jack said.

"Well, how often do you and Tess do it?" Bobby asked.

"This week, not at all," he replied with a chuckle.

"Come on, I'm serious. I need a comparison."

"There's no way I'm having this conversation with you. Tess and I both keep our private lives private."

"It's not like I'm going to tell anyone. Besides, Gina said she talks about this stuff with Tess and Luciana all the time."

"I know Tess. I can't believe she would talk to anyone about our sex life."

Bobby shrugged. "Dude, I'm telling you, Gina says they talk about it all the time. You know how women are, they talk about all kinds of stuff, including us, hell, probably mostly us. Gina told me that Luciana said that Joe's conservative in life, but not in bed. I mean, where else would I get that information?" he asked, chugging his beer.

Joe smiled, looked down, and laughed.

Bobby turned to Jack and said, "Just tell me, how often do you guys do it?"

"I can't believe we're having this conversation, but since you need help, I'll tell you. But again, what's normal for each couple is totally different."

"Yeah, well?" Bobby prodded.

"Once or twice a day, usually," Jack replied.

Bobby's jaw hit the floor. "You have sex every single day? Sometimes more than once?"

Jack nodded. "Except for the week around when her father died and she was depressed, and then for about a month after her car accident when she was recovering. And now this week. But yeah, other than that, usually once or twice a day. Sometimes more in Hawaii."

"No wonder you two are so freaking happy all the time," Bobby said.

"We're not happy this week."

Bobby lowered his voice and leaned closer. "What about blow jobs?"

"I am *not* having this conversation with you. We're not frat buddies."

"Come on. Just tell me. How often?"

Jack sighed with exasperation. "Once or twice a week. But that's it; I'm not telling you anything else."

Bobby's eyes were like saucers. "You get blow jobs every week. I hate you. Try once or twice a year for me. Usually just on my birthday," he said, guzzling his beer.

Jack and Joe laughed.

"Guys, I'm telling you for real, I'm freaking out. I love Gina and I don't want anyone else, but we're in a serious rut and it's only getting worse. I don't know how to get her more interested."

"I'm probably the last person who should be giving relationship advice since my wife isn't even speaking to me, but here's a wild idea: try talking to Gina about it instead of harassing the two of us," Jack said.

"Here, here," Joe said, raising his beer bottle. "To talking with our women and not dragging our friends into it."

They all clinked bottles.

Joe threw his arm up to signal to the waitress that they wanted another round.

"Jack, you gotta work it out with Tess. You're living the dream. Don't screw it up," Bobby said.

Jack huffed. "I'd be happy if she'd just hold my hand and look at me the way she used to."

* * *

Jack walked into the house and found Tess sitting on the couch, reading, her legs outstretched.

She looked at him, took her glasses off, and put her book on the coffee table. "Hey," she said quietly.

"Hey," he said.

He walked over, sat on the edge of the couch, and put his hand on her leg.

"Did you have a good time?" she asked.

He shrugged. "I missed you."

"Me too. Did you drink a lot?"

"No, just a couple of beers."

She scrunched her legs up and moved closer to him.

"Tess, I want to say something to you but I'm terrified you'll leave."

"I promise I won't. I wanted to talk to you, too."

"Really?" he asked, a look of hope flashing across his face. "What did you want to talk about, sweetheart?"

"You go first."

"Tess, I promised that if you came home, I'd keep my distance and give you all the space you need. I will, for as long as it takes if that's truly what you want." He paused and put his hands on her knees. "But if there's something I can do to make this better, anything, please tell me. You seem so unhappy and I don't want you to think I'm not fighting for us."

"Jack, I thought it would be easier like this. I'm not ready to talk about Lenny or what you did. I need time to sort through things in my own mind first, to figure out how I really feel about it and what I need from you. And since I can't give you what you want, I didn't think it was fair for me to ask for anything else, but..."

"What is it, sweetheart?" he asked, his arms wrapped around her knees.

"For me, living this way is hell on earth. I miss you. I just want to feel close to you again," she said softly.

"Me too, baby," he said, tears in his eyes.

She used her thumbs to gently wipe his tears and then rested her hand on his cheek. He cupped her face in his hands. They both leaned forward and kissed lightly. They pressed their foreheads together.

"Oh Tess," he whispered, a tear falling down his face. "I love you so much."

"I love you, too."

"Baby, please tell me we're going to be together."

"Jack…"

"It's okay," he said, rubbing her cheeks and then pulling his head back to look into her eyes. "I'm sorry. I know you can't say that now."

"Jack, I can tell you that trying to imagine a life without you has been the most painful thing I've ever experienced. I love you more than anything in the world. I want to be with you forever, but I just don't know right now. I'm not ready."

"That's okay. It's okay," he whispered, gently pulling her head to his, touching forehead to forehead again.

After a moment passed, she drew slightly back and looked into his eyes. "I'm not angry with you anymore. It's more complicated than that now. What I want is to spend time with you like we always do, to feel close to you. I'm not ready to talk about what happened yet, but I want to talk about everything else, to share as much as we can. I know I'm not always good at that, but I'll try."

"I want that, too," he said. "All I want is to feel close to you, to be with you. I promise I won't pressure you. Take all the time you need."

"When we fell in love, we agreed not to delve into everything in our pasts, to not push each other. We just accepted each other, with all of our problems, no questions. That was so beautiful. I never wanted to lose that, but now I feel like we need to talk about some of those things."

"Tess, sharing is beautiful, maybe even more beautiful because it's another way of being close. We won't lose anything. What we have is so special."

"We need to be totally honest with each other. There's nothing without trust. It means everything to me. Please promise me you won't hold anything back, even if it's difficult or you don't think it's what I want to hear."

"I give you my word."

She smiled faintly. "Thank you. And Jack?"

"What is it baby?"

"We can't make love. Even if we want to, we can't. The reason it's always been so special between us is because from the first night we met, I trusted you completely. Every time we're together, I see only you. Right now, the things in my mind are a jumbled mess. Until I sort through it, I just can't."

"I understand. It's okay, sweetheart," he said, stroking the side of her face. "I just want to be near you."

"Jack, if we're together like that before we move through all of this, it could forever change things between us in a way we'll never be able to repair. You have to trust me. We really can't be intimate in that way, and I know how we are when we spend time together. I mean, even right now, every part of me wants to be with you," she said, caressing the side of his face. "But it could irreparably damage what we have. Do you understand?"

"I do. I always want you too, but I can control myself. My eyes are entirely focused on the big picture. I'm not going to let anything happen that would hurt you or make it less likely that we're together because, Tess, I know you don't know it right now, but in my heart, in my whole heart, I know we belong together. I will do everything in my power to make it easy for you to choose us."

She leaned forward and they kissed tenderly. "I love you so much," she whispered.

"I love you, too. More than I could ever say."

"Come on," she said, scooting back. "Lie down and tell me what's going on with Joe and Bobby."

They both lay down. Jack put his arm around Tess, and she rested her head on his chest and draped her arm across his body.

"You have no idea how good this feels, just to hold you," he said.

"Yes, I do. It's like that for me too. So, tell me about your guys' night."

"Well, it was kind of a pity party. Everyone's having relationship issues."

"Joe and Luciana?" she asked.

"Yeah. Joe asked her to move in with him and she turned him down. I guess she's happy with how things are. Plus, he said she's concerned their schedules will clash."

"I get that. She's told me how she works, and it's definitely not nine to five. She's such a free spirit and so creative. She's probably worried that she'll have to sacrifice her process in some way, and if she does, that she'll resent him and it will ruin their relationship."

"Were you ever worried about that with us and your writing?"

She sat up to look at him. "Never. I felt like you accepted me exactly the way I am, like I did with you. Things were always easy with us. We could both just *be*. I knew you wouldn't try to change me or ask me to choose between writing and our relationship. Then, when I was writing *Ray of Light* and you stayed by my side, you confirmed every good thing I had always felt."

He put his hand on her cheek and she leaned forward to kiss him. She lay back down, her head on his chest.

"I was telling Joe tonight that I love watching you work. You have so much passion. I love seeing it, whether it's directed at me, one of your novels, your business, the charities you care about, or your friends. It's just all so beautiful. I'm constantly in awe of you."

"I've felt more creative and freer since I met you. It's been an enormous gift. Maybe it could be that way for Luciana, too."

"I hope so. Joe's crazy about her. I think they'll stay together anyway, but I'd love to see him have the kind of day-to-day happiness he longs for."

"What about Bobby? You said everyone was having relationship problems. Is it the sex thing?"

He rolled onto his side to face her. "Yes," he said with a laugh. "Bobby told me that you and the girls talk about this stuff, but I didn't believe him."

"Uh, hello? Have we met? Do you really think I talk about our sex life with anyone? Gina and Luciana talk about this stuff; I just listen."

"I knew it," he said. "You know he got me to share a bunch of stuff."

"He played you," she said with a giggle.

Jack leaned forward and kissed her. "I love seeing you smile."

"Is he really upset they're not, shall we say, as active as he might hope? Gina's pretty worried he's gonna leave her."

"He's definitely not going to leave her. He loves her and doesn't want anyone else, but he's a little frustrated. What's the deal?"

"Baby, do you know why we do it so much?"

"Because we can't keep our hands off each other," he replied, tucking her hair behind her ear.

She smiled. "Well, yeah, sort of. When you got home tonight, you sat on the edge of the couch, right next to me. You put your hand on my leg. Within a matter of minutes, you had touched my legs, my face, you had your arm around me, and you kissed me. You're always affectionate like that. It makes me feel so connected to you. Some men never touch their partners unless they want sex. Without that day-to-day intimacy, a lot of women have a hard time suddenly being in the mood with a snap of the fingers."

"Did Gina say that's what Bobby's like?"

"Pretty much. I mean, we spend a lot of time with them. Do you ever see them touching each other? He won't even dance with her. When we get in bed at night, we snuggle, we spoon, we wrap our arms around each other, we rub each other's fingers. Gina says that when Bobby gets in bed, he rolls onto his side, away from her, says 'goodnight,' and flips the lights off. She said the only time he does anything else is if he wants sex, after which he rolls over and goes to sleep without a word."

"Poor guy, he has no idea," Jack said.

"You have to help him."

"How did I get roped into this?"

"They're our friends and they love each other. Find a way to say something to him. Guide him in the right direction. I'm sure it's more complicated and that there's other stuff going on; I mean, they had that miscarriage, now they have a baby. I'm sure that all plays a role, too. And who knows? Maybe Gina isn't affectionate either. All I know is that a lot of women can't turn it on and off like that. If he wants more sex, he's going to have to be more physical when it's not sexual. Romance matters."

He grazed his fingers along her cheek. "Am I romantic enough with you?"

"Baby, you're the most romantic man I've ever met. I feel your love every second of every day."

"That's how you make me feel. It's not about sex. Making love with you is bliss, but I've told you before that what I love most is showing you how I feel about you. There are other ways to do that," he said, stroking her hair.

She smiled.

"You know I would never want you to do anything you don't want to do," he said.

"Let me guess—he complained about the no blow job thing."

Jack cracked up. "He might have mentioned it. What's that about?"

Tess shrugged. "Same thing, probably. Plus I don't think she likes doing it."

"And you do, with me?"

"There's nothing that makes me happier than making you happy. It's the best feeling. Besides, pleasing you turns me on."

"I feel the same way." He leaned forward and pressed his lips to hers. "But sweetheart, since we're abstaining for the foreseeable future, I think we need to change the topic or there won't be a cold enough shower in the world."

She giggled. "It's so hard to feel distant from you and so easy to feel close; it's the most natural thing. I know we have a lot to work through and that things aren't certain or easy, but Jack, I can't tell you how glad I am to feel close to you again."

"Me too, sweetheart," he said, hugging her tightly.

CHAPTER 12

The next morning, Tess woke up curled up against Jack, his arm across her waist.

"Hey," she whispered.

"Good morning, sweetheart. How'd you sleep?"

"Like a log. No nightmares."

He kissed the side of her head and she nuzzled into him.

They lay quietly for a few minutes and Tess said, "Want to go for a run?"

"Sure."

They got up, changed into running clothes, and headed into the kitchen. Jack poured two glasses of orange juice and handed one to Tess.

She put it down on the counter. "I just want water. Thanks anyway."

"Sweetheart, you've barely eaten for days. How about just a little juice before we go out?"

She looked at him, sadness in her eyes.

He rubbed her shoulders and softly said, "I know it's hard for you right now and I don't want to push, but I'm worried you're going to pass out. Please try."

She picked up the glass, drank half of it, and placed it back on the counter.

"Thank you, baby," he said, kissing her forehead. He gulped his juice and they headed out.

***

"Oh my God, I'm dripping," Jack said as they barreled into the kitchen, both out of breath. "I didn't think you were ever going to turn back." He grabbed two bottles of water and tossed one to Tess. They both guzzled them.

After downing her bottle, Tess wiped her brow and said, "It felt great to just *go*."

"I'm starving. Let's shower and make breakfast."

She looked at him like a deer in headlights. He put his hand on her arm. "I'll use one of the guest bathrooms, and you can use ours. Meet you back here?"

She smiled and said, "See you in a bit."

When Tess was ready, she found Jack in the kitchen pouring coffee. He handed her a mug.

"Thanks," she said.

"What do you feel like? Oatmeal? Or I can make something else."

"Oatmeal is good."

"We still have some blueberries in the fridge if you want to grab them," he said.

She got the blueberries and washed them while Jack made the oatmeal. Just as he was about to spoon it into the bowls, she stopped him. "Wait, don't do mine," she said.

She rummaged around in a drawer and took out the measuring cups. She put the one-cup measure back in the drawer and then started fiddling with the quarter-, third-, and half-cup measures, eventually selecting the third-cup size and putting the others away.

"Tess, that's not enough food," Jack said. "You usually have a cup, and you haven't measured it in years."

"Please just leave me be," she said defensively.

He came up behind her and put his hands on her hips. "I love you," he whispered. He brushed her hair aside, kissed her neck, and stepped out of her way.

She stuck the third-cup scoop into the pot, retrieved her portion, and dumped it into her bowl.

"How about some berries?" he asked.

She looked hesitantly at the berries sitting on the counter on a paper towel. She started moving them around and counting. When she had made a pile of twelve berries, she scooped them up and dropped them into her bowl. Jack ladled a large portion into his bowl and topped it with a fistful of berries, and they went to sit on the couch.

Jack watched Tess take tiny bites of her food to make it last longer. When they were both done eating, he took her hand. Her stomach growled.

"Sweetheart, I know things are difficult, but I'm really worried about you. You need to eat more."

"I can't," she said.

"Why?"

"Because I'm afraid I'll disappear."

"I don't understand. Can you try to explain it to me? I've always thought your food issues were about control and especially trying to control your body, which is completely understandable with everything you've been through."

"It's more than that, Jack. The reason I try to eat as little as possible is the same reason I don't drink. Do you know how many book parties and award ceremonies there have been where everyone was toasting me and I didn't allow myself even a single sip of champagne? Not one sip, even though I wanted to?"

He interlaced his fingers with hers. "Why, baby?"

"When you feel hungry, you're totally aware of your body. You know that you're here, that you're alive. I know I'm here because I feel hungry. I don't drink because that numbs you and I'm terrified I won't know that I exist anymore. Growing up, I had to numb myself completely to survive the things they did to me. I didn't want to live my whole life that way. I wanted to feel everything, every moment, even the hard ones. So, I gave myself a way to know I'm still here. That's why I refused prescription meds after the car accident—I would rather feel pain than feel nothing."

"Oh Tess, come here," he said, leaning forward and embracing her. He rubbed the back of her head and whispered, "Let me help you."

Eventually, she pulled back.

"Do you remember the first weekend we spent together, at your old apartment?" she asked.

"Yes. Every minute of it."

"We ordered Chinese food and I was so happy that I stuffed myself silly. I didn't even realize what I'd done until it was too late. I hadn't felt full in so long and it made me feel completely panicked."

"You've been healthy for such a long time, almost our whole relationship."

"That was because of you." Her eyes glossed over with tears. "I didn't need to starve anymore. I knew I was here because of the way you saw me."

"Nothing has changed that," he said gently.

"Yes, it has," she said, tears falling down her cheeks.

He gently brushed away the salty water, and then placed his hand on her cheek.

"What you said to me, that he ruined my life, is that how you see me? Is that how you've always seen me since our first night together? All these years? Do you think I'm ruined?" she asked, tears cascading down her face. She sniffled and continued, "I always thought we both knew the other had experienced pain and that we somehow fit together because of it. I never imagined you saw me as broken. You promised me that you'd be honest, so you have to tell me—is that really how you see me?"

"No, baby. I swear to you. I've never thought that for a second," he said, stroking her cheek. "What I said came out all wrong. I'm sorry that I made you doubt the way that I see you. I hate him for what he did to you. It's unspeakable. That any man could do that to anyone, but you, Tess, my sweet Tess, that he did that to *you*, I don't have the words to tell you how that makes me feel. He stole something from you; something that should never be taken from anyone. It's excruciating to know I can never change that for you. But you are not ruined or broken. I've never seen you that way. You are the strongest, most beautiful, accomplished, awe-inspiring person I've ever met. *That* is how I see you. It always has been."

She leaned into his hand. "Jack, you have such a deep desire to protect people, and I'm just afraid that's what you saw in me: someone who needed to be protected."

"Baby, of course I want to protect you, but that's not why I fell so crazy in love with you. From our first night together, I wanted to take care of you and I wanted you to take care of me. I still do. I promise you. I'm so sorry for what I said. It was out of rage and feeling defensive. But sweetheart, if you just look into my eyes, you'll know how I see you, how I've always seen you. I admire you more than I could ever put into words. Truthfully, it was less that I wanted to save you and more that I knew you could save me."

She wiped her face and burrowed into him. He wrapped his arms around her and whispered, "I see you, Tess Miller, who you really are. You're here, and I know it."

***

A little while later, Jack asked, "Are you working today, or do you want to do something?"

"Oh, work. That reminds me, I'm supposed to have my weekly video conference with my team today. It's not until this afternoon, so we could do something beforehand. What do you have in mind?"

"It's a gorgeous day and the farmers market is open. We could get a couple of those fresh limeades you love and stroll around. Walking in the sunshine and holding your hand would make my day. Maybe we could stop at a stand or two and buy some food. There's barely anything to eat in the house. I know you love the produce there. You can see what looks good, what's in season. We could cook together tonight if you want."

"That sounds perfect. I'll go put my shoes on."

Two hours later, they trudged into the kitchen carrying three canvas bags overflowing with fruits and vegetables. They were laughing uproariously.

"I'm telling you, that woman with the pies was definitely flirting with you. And right in front of me. Pretty brazen," Tess said.

"She was just trying to sell us pie. That's why she gave me so many samples," Jack replied.

"She was offering a lot more than a sample of pie."

Jack put the bags on the counter and grabbed Tess's waist. "Well, too bad for her. I'm already taken. I like it that you're jealous, though."

"I'm always jealous when women come on to you."

They stood smiling at each other, sparks flying between them. After a moment passed, Jack cleared his throat and said, "Well, we should unpack." He opened the refrigerator and started putting the food away. "What should I leave out for later?"

"How about we make the eggplant tonight and the soup tomorrow?"

"Sounds good. I'm hungry. Want some lunch?"

"Sure. Toss me the kale and mint and I'll make a salad."

Tess made a kale salad with fresh mint, cannellini beans, and pine nuts, dressed in lemon juice and olive oil. Jack handed her two plates, a roll on his. She stood with tongs in her hand, thinking about how to parcel out the salad. Jack saw her struggling and walked over. He kissed her on the cheek. "I love you," he whispered. "It's okay. Just do what you can and don't fret."

She smiled and placed a large mound of salad on his plate and a medium-sized mound on hers. He pecked her cheek again. They plopped down on barstools at the counter, where Jack had placed two sparkling waters. Halfway through their meal, Tess's phone rang. Jack slid it over to her.

"Omar's calling. I should answer."

"Do you want privacy?"

"No baby, it isn't like that," she said, putting her hand on his arm.

She swiped to answer the call. "Hey, Omar. You're on speakerphone and Jack is here. We're in the middle of lunch. What's up?"

"Hello, Butterfly. Hi, Jack."

"Hi, Omar."

"I wanted to remind you that we have our weekly team call today, but if it's not good for you, of course we can reschedule, although the legal team does need to speak with you urgently."

"I remembered the call. It's fine. I know there are a lot of time-sensitive things going on. We can have the meeting. But thanks for checking."

"How are you guys doing?"

Tess rubbed Jack's arm and looked at him lovingly. "We're doing better. Working on things."

"I'm so glad to hear it."

"How are you and Clay?" Tess asked.

"Do you mean was I furious with him for calling me out on my shit?"

She giggled. "Something like that."

"No, we're fine. I know what he said has merit. Sometimes when you love someone so much, it's hard to remember that they can take care of themselves and don't always need you. I've only ever wanted to look out for you, as you have always done for me. I never meant to make you feel like I don't properly respect you. Nothing could be further from the truth."

"I know. And I love you."

"Go on, finish your lunch. We'll be starting the group call in an hour."

"Bye, Omar."

"Bye, Butterfly."

Jack looked at Tess and touched her hand. "Tess, what Omar said to you, the same is true for me. I love you so much that sometimes I can't see straight. I just want to take care of you and make you feel the way you make me feel. I know I've made mistakes. I own them. I will do better."

"Everyone makes mistakes. They make us human. You told me something like that a long time ago," she said.

"It's never been that I don't respect you, and I'm so sorry that it seemed that way. There's no one I respect more."

She rubbed his fingers, smiled faintly, and said, "Thank you." She picked up her fork and finished her salad.

***

An hour later, Tess said, "I'm going up to the office for the video chat. Jack…"

"Yeah?"

"Will you come with me? My mind has been on other things. It would be good to have another set of ears in the room."

He smiled. "Of course."

They headed upstairs, hand in hand. Tess grabbed a notepad, pen, her reading glasses, and laptop. She set up the laptop on the coffee table at the far end of the room. They plopped down on the couch. A minute later, her legal team, her accountant Barry, her assistant Crystal, and Omar were all on the line.

"Hi, Butterfly. We're all here. Andy would like to begin with the legal report, if that's all right with you, which will piggyback onto a licensing issue I need to address."

"Good afternoon, everyone. Yes, that's fine. Jack is with me," she replied.

"Tess, we finally got word back on our trademark applications," Andy said.

"Hang on, I want to fill Jack in," Tess replied. She turned to Jack. "I think you know I have registered trademarks for some of my most well-known characters, which is part of how I've been able to broker such good entertainment and merchandising deals."

"Yes," he replied.

"For a long time, I've wanted to trademark the popular phrases in my novels, those that have become recognizable sayings in the culture. Historically, authors have been able to get trademarks for their characters and titles of serials, but not their writing. Songwriters have had more success trademarking lyrics. I wanted to push the issue. Artists of all mediums should own their work and control how it's used and monetized. They should have rights. I don't think I mentioned it to you at the time because it was such a long shot and we were in the middle of promoting my last novel."

"Got it," Jack said.

"Okay, Andy. What's the news?" Tess asked.

"It's awesome. We were issued twelve of the trademarks we applied for! I know we were going for fifteen, but as I'm sure you recall, that was largely strategy. I honestly didn't think we'd get any of them. This is a monumental victory for an author. Glad you pushed us," Andy said.

Tess looked at Jack and he grinned from ear to ear.

"Thank you, Andy, for fighting for this. Thanks to the whole team, really. Well done. That's terrific work. Did you use the arguments I suggested?" Tess asked.

"We did, including those media clips you sent and the social media hashtags. Brilliant ideas. I've emailed you the list of what we got, but I can also review it now if you like."

"No need, I'm reading your email on my phone. Please continue," she said, jotting down the phrases on her notepad.

"Tess, one of the upsides of getting these trademarks registered is that they increase our ability to go after folks who are unfairly profiting from your work. How aggressive would you like us to be?" Andy asked.

"I always believe it's best to devote our efforts to positivity, not negativity. Please just continue the normal monitoring. When you come upon infringements, send the standard cease and desist notice. Any issue that persists, please bring it to me before spending additional resources."

"Got it," Andy said. "I would argue with you, but I know there's no point."

Tess giggled. "Save your arguments for when someone violates a trademark. I look forward to sparring with you."

Andy laughed. "Omar is going to jump in now to discuss the media and licensing implications."

"Butterfly," Omar said, "This is going to become an international news story. You've broken new ground for authors. As we discussed when we filed for trademark protection, there will be those who see this as a huge victory for artists, and those who claim it's a money grab that will inhibit the artistic freedom of others. We have the statement you drafted at the time ready if you want to release it in response. How do you want to handle this?"

"Let's preemptively put out the statement. Under no circumstances do I want any comment from our camp beyond the prepared statement. I will not be publicly discussing it further. But that was drafted a while ago, so I'd like to review it first. I want Jack to read it too, so please email it to us both now."

"On it," Crystal said.

A moment later, Jack said, "Got it."

"Jack and I are going to review this. Please hang tight."

Tess and Jack both read the statement. "What do you think?" she asked him.

"It's good. I think it accomplishes what you want. My only suggestion is in the last paragraph, I would change the sentence about supporting artists to something like, 'in solidarity with other artists.' I think it makes it harder to attack you."

"Ooh, that's an excellent edit. Thank you. Everyone, did you hear that?"

"Yes, Butterfly. Got it. We're making the change and we'll get it out before the news hits tonight."

"Just remind me not to watch or read the news for the next week until the story passes," Tess said.

Omar smiled. "Butterfly, the question now is what we want to do with these registered trademarks. As you know, there are already two potential business partners interested in licensing deals. The first is that high-end jeweler. They'd like to do a series of engraved gold jewelry—lockets, charm bracelets, and so on. The other is that retail chain aimed at the teen and twenty-something market. They're envisioning diaries, backpacks, messenger bags, buttons, and costume jewelry, although their stock varies so widely, I think they're open to collaborating. They both want you to be a spokesperson for the line and would love to feature your image on store displays. I'm not sure yet if that's negotiable. From our talks to date, I'm imagining we could get similar terms from either. You may want to hear from Barry directly, but the gist is that both offer similar long-range financial forecasts. What are your thoughts?"

"I need some time to think about it. To be candid, I have reservations."

"Obviously, you can take whatever time you want, but we pursued these trademarks in part for these very kinds of opportunities. Would you like to share your reservations?" Omar asked.

"The motivations behind my work and my choices have never been money. There's always been an artistic or social purpose. Until I can figure out what that is, I'm holding on to the trademarks. But I do have a question for legal."

"Yes?" Andy said.

"I realize either of these companies will demand exclusive rights, but can we control the term for the license? And if so, how many years are we talking about? It's important to me that I ultimately own those sayings again, in both copyright and trademark."

"Good question, Tess. Yes, we will control the term. We don't know what they'll ask for until they send a draft contract. My best guess is anywhere from five to ten years. Assuming they're playing hardball, it will be on the higher end."

"Omar, I don't want any promises made or implied because I need to mull this over, but I'll tell you now that I'm not comfortable with a term that exceeds seven years. My strong preference is for three to five years, the lower the better, with an option to renew on a biannual basis, mutually agreed upon and in writing. Why don't you reach out to them and see what they'd be willing to accept? Play them off each other. Please make it clear that I want to be involved with creative. This will be a true collaboration. These phrases won't appear on anything I haven't approved."

"Okay, Butterfly. I'm on it. Shall we move on to other licensing matters? I have a list of reprint requests that need your approval."

"Sure thing. I'm listening," she said, pen in hand.

They spent the next half hour reviewing licensing deals. At the end, Omar said, "Okay Butterfly, there are just two more things on our agenda."

"Go ahead."

"With all of your recent press, Hollywood has come calling again. There's going to be a major entertainment deal coming our way any day. I'd actually hoped to have it in hand for this meeting."

"Yeah, I've heard whispers too, but only that it's for a limited series from the same platform we sold to last time. Which book do they want? Do you have any more details?"

Omar shook his head. "They're being very hush-hush. From what I hear, they're trying to line up A-list stars before approaching us. They're looking for an award winner. We have some guesses about which book, but I'd be hesitant to say."

"Well, what are you thinking?"

"Honestly, I really don't want to get your head spinning when it's only a guess."

"Do you remember the conversation we had earlier, Omar? Please tell me."

"Sorry, Butterfly. We suspect it'll be *Morning Sun*. I think they're courting controversy for ratings. It's also one of the only books that hasn't been made into a movie or television series, and we've heard some rumors. I know that may be challenging for you."

Tess inhaled deeply.

"Again, we don't actually know. There's also a chance it could be *Holiday Homes* or *Ray of Light*, the latter of which I know you want to keep pure as a novel. Tess, there really is no point in going down that road until we know for sure."

"You said there were two final licensing issues. What's the other one?"

"The licensing terms for all foreign translations to three of your novels will expire in ninety-nine days. As you know, we have to inform them at least ninety days before the term expires if we want to renew for another five years. All thirty-two publishers want to renew each of the three books. Bravo."

"Let me guess, *Morning Sun* is one of them."

"Yes."

"I'm not renewing any contracts until we know more about this potential entertainment deal. I've heard the rumors too, and I think we'll get an offer any day now. We have nine days left to renew. I'm willing to take my chances. If we sign an entertainment deal for any of the books they're after, we can renegotiate all of those contracts, double or even triple the non-recoupable licensing fees."

"I thought you'd say that. I would be remiss not to tell you that everyone on the team is a little concerned about the rapidly approaching deadline."

"Well, I'm not. Nothing ventured, nothing gained. I've never been afraid of risk, and I'm not going to start now. What I am afraid of is underselling my work because we made a fear-based decision. I will not be guided by fear. If the licenses run out, we'll all survive.

According to the report Barry sent over, we've made some very smart investments and we're now worth over six hundred million, despite his endless concerns over my charitable giving. No one is going to starve if those books go out of print abroad. But because I can see the sweat glistening on your brow, let me remind you that I don't think that will happen. We will make the deadline. So the final word on the matter is that we wait."

"Alright, Butterfly. Anything on your agenda before we go?"

"Just a question for accounting. Barry, did you take care of those matters we discussed the other day?"

"Yes. The deposit will go through first thing tomorrow morning, and the mortgages should clear next week."

"Thank you. Good work everyone. I think that's it. Please send my best to your families. Bye."

She turned her computer off and inhaled deeply.

"Wow. That was amazing," Jack said. "Tess, this is exactly what I was saying earlier. I'm completely in awe of you. That trademark victory is incredible. Listening to you run that meeting, how brilliant you are, how powerful and bold and unafraid, even when I know how much you're going through right now. You are the strongest, most capable person I know. Don't ever let anything stupid I say make you doubt that."

"It's just work, it's not a big deal. Thank you for helping."

He shook his head. "You are remarkable. What you've built and the way you run your empire, well, it's extraordinary. Don't diminish it." He held her hand. "Tess, I need you to know that I see everything you are. I love you for all of it, for how you are so powerful and still so capable of vulnerability."

"That's how I feel about you," she said, rubbing his fingers.

"What was that last thing about mortgages? Have we bought a new home I should know about?"

She looked down.

"What is it?" he asked.

"When I was staying at Omar and Clay's, I asked Barry to deposit half a million dollars into your parents' bank account and to pay off your siblings' mortgages."

"What?" he asked, his eyes wide.

"In case we don't end up together, I wanted to make sure your family is taken care of. I mean, you'd have plenty of money to do it because I would never sign that ridiculous prenup, but I wanted to do something for them myself."

"Oh, Tess. Come here, baby," he said, opening his arms.

She burrowed into him.

"You are the most generous human being I've ever met. I can't believe you were thinking about them when you were in so much pain. Not just generous in money, but so deeply generous in spirit."

"I love your family."

"They're your family, too. So am I. Forever."

She looked up at him and he stroked her cheek. He leaned forward and they kissed tenderly. She rested her head on his chest, enveloped in his strong arms. "We are going to be together, sweetheart. I know it in my heart. I can't lose you. I love you so much."

"I love you too," she whispered.

***

"It smells good," Tess said as Jack pulled the grilled, no-breading eggplant parmesan out of the oven. "What do you want to drink?" she asked.

"I already set the table in the dining room for us, when you were changing into your pajamas."

"The dining room?" she asked.

"I wanted to make it nice. You have a huge win to celebrate. Grab the salad and go sit down. I'll be right behind you with the plates."

"Jack, please don't give me too much. I'm…"

"It's okay. I'll just give you a little. Eat what you want."

She smiled and grabbed the salad bowl. She walked into the dining room to see the table covered in glowing votive candles.

Jack walked in behind her and set her plate down. As promised, he'd only served her a modest portion of food.

"It's so pretty in here. You didn't have to go to all this trouble."

"It's no trouble," he said, kissing the top of her head. He sat down and picked up his sparkling water. "Cheers, baby. Congratulations on your trademark victory. I'm so proud of you."

"Thanks," she said, clinking her glass to his. She served him some salad and then put a little on the side of her plate.

He began eating. Tess just sat, looking down at her plate.

"So, I was thinking about those two licensing offers you have in front of you. If they both come back with short terms like you want, do you know which you're leaning toward?"

"I always liked the idea of partnering with the lower-end chain that caters to young people. My messages are all meant to be empowering, which is why I wanted to protect them. I'd love to see them as mantras for young women. I have ideas for things we could do, but the whole thing leaves me feeling uneasy. Even though I believe in the messages, it still feels like a money grab, which makes me uncomfortable. It's too commercial."

"Let's brainstorm," he said.

"Okay," she replied, picking up her fork and taking a small bite of eggplant.

"What if you partnered with a charity you care about?" he suggested.

"I would love that, but I haven't thought of anything that makes sense. Honestly, I spent so much time with the lawyers, crafting the arguments for the trademarks, knowing that it was probably for nothing, that I didn't spend enough time thinking about the next step."

"Well, they were talking about a line of backpacks and diaries. I've heard about charities that donate backpacks with school supplies to kids in need, both here in the US and abroad. If you look overseas, there may even be opportunities to work directly with girls' schools."

Tess smiled brightly. "That's such a fantastic idea. Maybe something like, 'For every x amount spent here, we donate a backpack filled with school supplies.' We could use our own bags with the mantra embroidered on them."

"I can do some research tomorrow if you want, see what kinds of charities are already set up for this. I'm sure you could get Crystal and Omar to look into it as well."

"Jack," she said softly.

"Yeah, baby?"

She reached out and rested her hand on his. "Thank you, that's all."

"What for?"

"For always understanding and being there."

He smiled.

They continued talking and eating. Tess scraped her plate clean.

CHAPTER 13

At four in the morning, Tess woke up like a bolt, screaming at the top of her lungs.

Jack sprang up and threw his arms around her. "It's okay, sweetheart. It's okay. I'm here. I'm here and I love you."

She was rocking back and forth, her body heaving, her breathing labored. Jack held her tightly.

"It's not my fault. It's not my fault," she gasped.

"No baby, it's not your fault." He held her closely, slowing his own breathing to encourage her to do the same.

"He did such awful things. Make it stop," she whimpered.

"I'm so sorry, sweetheart," he said, cradling her, one arm around her back and the other around her head. "I've got you. You're safe now. I'll do anything for you."

"It's not my fault," she wheezed.

"No sweetheart, none of it is your fault."

After a few minutes passed, Tess's breathing steadied.

"Come here, baby," Jack said, helping her lie down. She put her face against his chest, and they flung their arms over each other. "I love you so much, with my whole heart, forever," he whispered.

Eventually, they fell back asleep.

Tess woke up a little after seven o'clock, still pressed firmly against Jack. He was already awake, staring at her. He gently brushed the side of her head. "I love you," he said softly.

"I love you, too." After a few peaceful minutes passed, she said, "It sounds like it's raining."

"Yeah, it is."

"I had hoped to go for a run. Do you want to go up to the gym for a workout instead?"

"Sure, sweetheart," he said, kissing the side of her head.

They took turns using the bathroom and headed upstairs. Tess jumped on the treadmill. She ran at a high speed for an hour, while

Jack moved from machine to machine. She was drenched when she finally stopped.

"I'll shower up here again. Meet you in the kitchen for breakfast?" Jack said.

She nodded.

When Tess made it to the kitchen, Jack had already made coffee and oatmeal. He was about to ladle it into their bowls, but stopped to ask, "How much do you want, sweetheart?"

She opened the drawer with the measuring cups and silently took out the third-cup measure. He took it from her and said, "Okay."

They sat at the counter eating. Jack watched as Tess again slowly nibbled on her food. When she was done eating, he put his hand on hers and said, "I know it's difficult right now, but it will get better. I promise I'll help you. I don't expect anything in return."

She smiled dimly. "I really do love you."

"I know. I love you, too."

She got up and carried their bowls to the dishwasher. She turned and looked at Jack, tears in her eyes.

"Hey, what's this about?" he said, scurrying over and using his thumbs to wipe her tears away.

"I'm sorry," she said softly.

"For what? You have nothing to be sorry for."

"That I can't just forget—him, you, all of it. That I can't just forget or pretend and be better, make everything better."

"I don't expect you to do that," he said, draping his arms around her. "Nobody does. You always say the only way out is through. We're in the middle of it. I know you're trying. I can see it. That's all you can do. None of this is your fault. None of it, Tess."

She sniffled. After a moment passed, she said, "I'm gonna go upstairs and work. I'm behind on everything."

"Okay, sweetheart. I'm going to spend some time investigating charities like we talked about last night."

She smiled. "Thank you," she said, and she started to walk away. Before leaving the room, she stopped, turned, and said, "How about we make the soup together at lunchtime?"

"Find me whenever you're ready."

***

Around noon, Tess wandered downstairs and found Jack sitting on a kitchen barstool, scrolling away on his laptop.

"Hey there," she said softly.

"Hey, sweetheart. How's it going?"

"Good. I've been playing with the new trademarks we have. Working on different ideas for how to use them."

"I found a bunch of charities that do the type of thing we were talking about. I've been researching each one to check out how trustworthy they are. I have a list of suggestions with some comments I can email to Crystal and Omar if you like."

"That would be great. Thank you so much."

"My pleasure. You hungry? Ready to make some soup?"

She nodded.

They put on some quiet music and started on the soup. Jack washed the vegetables while Tess cut the onions. As usual, her eyes started to tear.

"Don't touch your face or it will sting," he said. He used his fingers to gently wipe under her eyes.

"Thank you, baby," she said, staring into his eyes.

"I always offer to do the onions," he said.

"Well if I let you do them, then you wouldn't come over and be so sweet."

He brushed her hair out of her face and she smiled. They both leaned forward and started to kiss, first gently and then with increasing passion. They grabbed each other's heads, running their fingers through each other's hair, kissing fervently. After a couple of minutes, Tess pulled back. They were both panting.

"I'm sorry. I'm sorry," Jack said, unable to meet her gaze.

She touched his hand. "Don't be sorry. But I can't."

He looked into her eyes, cupped her cheek in his hand, and said, "I know, baby."

She smiled, squeezed his hand, and said, "Let's make the soup."

An hour later, they were each slurping their last spoonful.

"That was so good. I'm gonna get more. Can I bring you anything?" Jack asked.

"I'm good, thanks."

Just as Jack jumped up to get more soup, Tess's phone rang. "Omar's FaceTiming," she said. "Hey, Omar. Did you get the charity info Jack sent over?"

"I did. We're going to look into all of it. Butterfly, I'm calling with news."

"What's up?"

"I know you just want me to be direct with you, but I'm still allowed to love you and be concerned. I'm a little leery of telling you this with everything going on. I understand the timing is dreadful."

Jack walked over and sat on the stool next to Tess.

"Please, just tell me," she said.

"We got the entertainment offer. It is for a limited television series, and it's a world-class deal. I'll email you the details as soon as we get off the line. As rumored, they already have A-list movie stars interested, including a few of your favorites. They're looking to fast-track the whole thing. Unfortunately, they want an initial response from us in five business days. Of course we can always tell them that isn't enough time, though I do want to remind you that we're down to eight days for the foreign translation renewals. You were smarter than all of us, as usual. You were right to wait."

Tess took a breath. "It's *Morning Sun*, right? That's what you don't want to tell me. They want *Morning Sun*."

He nodded. "Do you have any initial thoughts, or do you want to think about it and get back to me?"

"Omar, I have to go."

"Butterfly…"

"I have to go," Tess said, hanging up. She doubled over and started to heave. She jumped up and sprinted to her bathroom, Jack following. She knelt in front of the toilet. Jack held her hair with one hand and rubbed her back with the other. She vomited twice and then reached to flush the toilet.

"It's okay, sweetheart. It's okay," Jack said softly.

She sat up and muttered, "I need to brush my teeth and take a shower."

"I'll wait in our room. Call me if you need anything."

***

Tess emerged twenty minutes later. She grabbed Jack's hand. "Please come upstairs with me. I need to talk to you."

Without a word spoken, they went to the office. Tess walked to the bookcase where she displayed first editions of her novels. She pulled *Morning Sun* off the shelf and led Jack to the window seat. She sat, her legs outstretched, and he sat opposite her, his legs outstretched too.

"Do you remember when we first met and you bought all of my novels?"

"Yes. You told me to skip that one. At the time, I thought it was because you didn't like it as much as the others. That wasn't the reason, was it?"

She shook her head. "It's the book I'm most proud of. It's also the most personal. Omar is the only person who knows the truth of it. Everything in the book is so disguised that even the people who inspired it wouldn't recognize themselves. Of everything I've written, it's the most misunderstood and the most understood, which I know probably doesn't sound like it makes sense."

He put his hand on her ankle. "Explain it to me."

"It's about domestic violence and sexual assault. Really, it's about all the violence and abuse that happens to people in their own homes, behind closed doors. The protagonist is being battered by her husband. She loves him and doesn't want to lose him, but she's afraid he's going to kill her. So she decides to teach him how to beat her. She convinces him it's so others won't see the injuries and so she can heal faster, for the next round. She gives him lessons on how to batter her effectively. He goes along with it. Then the violence escalates and becomes sexual. He wants to hit her and fuck her in one go. So again, she teaches him. Throughout the whole book, he beats her and rapes her, over and over again, following her rules."

"Jesus."

"Yeah, it's really dark. In the middle of the book, there are thirteen straight pages that describe assault after assault in brutal detail. I broke every rule writing that book. I did everything they warned me not to do. You should have seen the folks at my publishing house when I delivered the manuscript. They begged me to change it, said it would ruin my career. Claire understood and defended me when I refused to water it down. It's one of the reasons I'm loyal to her."

"What happened when it was released?"

"It was the most polarizing thing I've ever published, which I expected. Some reviewers said it promoted domestic violence, rape, and victim blaming. They thought it was appalling, disgusting. Other reviewers, the ones who understood what I was really doing, said it was one of the bravest novels ever written. They commended me. One reviewer even called it, 'The Most Heartbreakingly Honest Book of the Century.' It won awards, which caused all kinds of controversy. I did book signings, but to this day I've never done a reading for it or any kind of media."

"And readers?"

"They embraced it wholeheartedly. They understood. Not just women either, but abuse survivors of all kinds. When I was touring the Middle East, it's the book women most often commented on. Do you remember that night at Shelby's when that Middle Eastern woman wanted to speak with me and Omar translated?"

He nodded.

"She told me about a friend's daughter who was gang raped. She talked about how much *Morning Sun* meant to the women in her community, that they knew I understood, and that they felt less alone for it. Readers rarely say these things in front of others, but when we're alone, it's the novel they most often thank me for, and the one that inspires them to tell me their stories. You see, my readers have always understood what the book is really about. It didn't claim to portray what domestic violence, rape, or incest survivors do, but how they might *feel*. You feel complicit. You feel as if, in some way, to some degree, it's your fault. Every time you cover a bruise, make an excuse, or don't tell what's happening to you, you feel complicit, as if you had given them a road map and your permission for them to violate you. I wrote it as a way to tell survivors that their trauma isn't their fault. They could not have changed what happened. They could not have controlled it. You don't have control when someone is hurting you. I wrote it to help people let go of their shame and learn to forgive themselves."

"Why didn't you want me to read it?"

"You had just told me about all the violent acts you were forced to perform for your job. It was obviously hard for you to talk about. *Morning Sun* is a stream of brutality, and I didn't want to drag you into it. I wanted to help you focus on good things. I was trying to bring light into your life, not more darkness."

"Come here," he said. They both scooched to the middle of the bench. He cupped her face in his hands. "You are so special, and I love you with all my heart."

She kissed him softly.

They leaned back.

"So, what happened to the protagonist?"

"Well, I told you I broke all the rules when I wrote this one."

"Yeah."

"Jack, she dies on the last page of the book. She's lying on her kitchen floor, the morning sun shining on her face, blood dripping onto the white linoleum."

"What happened?"

"He broke the rules."

***

"How about we watch a movie, have a bite, and snuggle on the couch?" Jack asked.

"Okay."

"We have leftover eggplant parm and soup, there's still a bunch of salad stuff, or we can get something delivered. What do you feel like?"

"I don't care. Let's just have leftovers. Heat up whatever you want."

"Grab some drinks and start looking for a movie. I'll bring the food in. Don't worry, I won't give you too much."

Tess was scrolling through movie choices when Jack placed two plates of eggplant parmesan and spinach salad on the coffee table.

"Just eat what you want," he said. "So, what are we watching?"

"Your choice. I vote for a comedy or something old."

"I would love to hear you laugh, so I say comedy."

Jack selected a film and they began eating. Tess took small bites, but as they became hysterical with laughter, she relaxed and cleaned her plate. She nestled into Jack until the movie ended.

"You're so pretty when you laugh. Your whole face lights up," Jack said.

She smiled. "I've always thought it's strange how human beings can go from emotion to emotion. Sometimes we're not even through with one, but it's like we get a respite. Our hearts can be heavy with sorrow, and yet something can make us smile, and temporarily lightens the darkness."

"Is that what it's like for you right now?"

"Yes. I can sit here and laugh with you, and it's real. But at the same time, I feel sad, confused, and overwhelmed."

He massaged her shoulders.

"It's hard enough trying to deal with everything that's happened, with Lenny, mostly with you, us. Now this thing with *Morning Sun*. I don't know how my head or my heart can hold space for all of these things."

"Tess, I understand the time constraints, but don't let anyone pressure you. If you need more time, take it. Everyone will deal with it. Remember, they all work for you."

"I know. Honestly, I believe the universe sends us messages, tries to help us when we need it. It's no coincidence this is happening now. That book has been out for more than a decade. Maybe this is all happening at once so that if I can get through it, I'll be past it. For good."

He caressed the palm of her hand. "Not if, when. I don't know how long it will take, or how much it will hurt, but you *will* get through all of this. I'll be here every step of the way. If you want me, if you'll have me, I'll be here forever."

She looked up at him, combed and smoothed his hair with her fingers, and kissed him.

"Sweetheart, I know I haven't read *Morning Sun*, but I've read your other novels. They may not be as dark as this one, but they're all raw, all full of pain. And yet, there's always hope that shines through in at least one of the characters."

She smiled. "Because people were so focused on how 'Tess Lee killed her protagonist,' most critics ignored the primary supporting character. She was also living with violence and shame, but she found a way to get out. She started dealing with it, confronting it, all of its horror and messiness. She was going to make it."

"Baby, sit up and look at me."

She sat up. He leaned forward, rubbed the tip of his nose to hers, and then planted a tiny kiss there. He pulled back, took her hands, and said, "You're going to make it too. And so will we."

Over the next three days, Tess woke up in the middle of the night, screaming. Jack comforted her. They went for runs in the morning, worked from home during the day, and spent time watching television, listening to music, and talking. Tess texted Omar telling him she needed time alone with Jack and that she'd be in touch when she was ready. She continued to measure and ration her food, but ate a little more each day. On the fourth day, something changed.

CHAPTER 14

Showered and dressed after a long run, Jack found Tess making breakfast in the kitchen.

"I finally beat you," she said, standing at the stove, stirring the oatmeal.

He walked over and put his hands on her waist.

"I put coffee out for you. Can you grab a couple of bowls, baby?" she said.

He pecked her cheek, retrieved the bowls from the cabinet, and plopped down on a barstool.

Tess switched off the burner. Jack watched as she put her hand on the drawer with the measuring cups. She stood for a moment, holding the knob, but then let it go. She took the serving ladle and scooped out two heaps for Jack and one for herself. He tried to mask his smile as she turned around and placed the bowls on the bar.

After breakfast, Jack said, "What do you want to do today? Are you going to work?"

"Actually, I kind of feel like going for a walk to get some air."

"Want some company?"

She put her hand on his. "If you don't mind, I'd like to be alone for a little while."

He stood up, grabbed their bowls, kissed the top of her head, and said, "Of course not."

She smiled and left.

***

Tess came home nearly three hours later. Jack was in the living room. He leapt up when he heard the door open. "Hey, I was getting worried about you."

"I'm sorry. I walked down to the park. Guess I lost track of time. I just needed to be by myself, to breathe and feel the sunlight on my skin."

He put his hand on her cheek and they stared at each other. "You all right?" he asked.

She nodded faintly.

"You hungry? I could make us lunch."

She shook her head. "Jack, I'm going up to the office. I have to read *Morning Sun*. I need you to leave me alone while I read it. Is that okay?"

"Yes. Anything you need."

She gently touched his hand, her fingers against his, and headed upstairs.

***

Jack was watching the news when Tess wandered into the living room just after five o'clock, a copy of *Morning Sun* in her hand. He flipped the television off but didn't get up.

"Hey, sweetheart. How are you doing?" he asked.

She sat down on the opposite end of the couch. "Once my books are published, I never read them again. I have excerpts from some that I read at book events, but that's it. I've never looked back at any of them before."

"What was it like, reading it?"

"It's so strange because for twenty years readers have been telling me how much my novels mean to them and how much they help them. I've never really understood that or been able to embrace it. My novels connect with readers because they resonate with their pain, and as you know, that's been very challenging for me. People say it's because it helps them through their pain, helps them feel not so alone, or it gives them hope or inspiration, but I've never been fully able to accept that. And now…"

He took her hand. "Now?"

"It helped me. Reading it helped me. It was comforting and clarifying, just like what people have always said it's done for them." She huffed.

He swept his fingers along the palm of her hand.

"Can I read you something?" she asked.

"Yes. I would love that."

"This part is from the end, when she's lying on the kitchen floor, gasping her last breaths, and she knows she's going to die. These are her dying thoughts.

"I just scrubbed the kitchen floor yesterday. Who will clean it when I'm gone? The stains will be awful. They'll need to use bleach. I wonder if a faint shadow will remain. Can stains ever really be scrubbed away? Are we ever clean? Why did he do that? Why didn't he follow the rules? Whose rules were they? I wanted them to be mine, but were they? Were they ever mine? I'm so cold. The sunshine feels good on my face. Maybe it will warm me from the outside in or the inside out. Maybe when they find me, I'll be a cold corpse with warm skin. I hope my ashes turn into a flower, like the flowers he gave me: the apology, the plea for forgiveness, after, between, before the next round. Maybe I'll be a flower with roots deep in the dark, cold ground, reaching far below anything they can see, a bloom desperate for the radiant warmth of the sun's love. I hope he doesn't come by and pluck me. I fear if he does, I'll forgive him. I always forgive him. Even now, in these last seconds, I don't know how to forgive myself."

As she finished reading, a tear slid down her face.

"Oh Tess," he said, reaching to wipe it away. "It's tragic, but beautiful and powerful."

She placed the book on the coffee table and looked straight into his eyes, resolute. "You've been so patient with me, and I appreciate that more than you know. Jack, I'm ready. I know how I feel and what I need from you. I'm ready to talk about it."

He straightened his body and inhaled deeply. His eyes locked to hers, he said, "Sweetheart, I love you. I'm listening."

"You look nervous," she said.

"I'm terrified. I'm terrified of losing you. But sweetheart, I want to hear anything you have to say. Please tell me."

"Jack, when you're hurt the way I was, you feel complicit. That's the worst agony of all of it. You keep replaying in your mind everything that was off before the abuse started. You think about every time they looked at you in a funny way, or got too close, or grazed your arm or leg. You think about all the things that didn't feel quite right, but that you ignored. Then, when things get bad, you wonder if you somehow allowed it. Your body starts to betray you. Most of the time it's awful and brutal, but sometimes you feel other things, physical things that you're confused by and ashamed to feel. At some point, it's less about what anyone has done to you, and more about how twisted you feel about yourself. Do you understand?"

"Yes," he said softly.

"Imagining a life without you is painful beyond words. You are the love of my life. I know that if we're not together, I will never recover. But as painful as that loss would be, there's something even worse: feeling complicit in violence. Feeling that way again, Jack, I wouldn't be able to live at all." She paused to wipe the wetness from her eyes. "I can't be with someone violent. It doesn't matter whether the violence is directed at me or someone else. It doesn't matter if they deserve it. My God, I'm vegetarian because I can't even harm an animal for food. I can't be a part of any kind of violence."

Jack's eyes welled. "Tess," he muttered, taking her hand.

"Please, let me finish," she said.

"I'm listening," he said softly, enormous tears falling from his eyes.

"I understand what you did to Lenny and the overwhelming rage you felt. I understand that hatred and how it was linked to your love for me. You didn't do anything I haven't thought of doing countless times myself. In your mind, you were defending me. I accept that. I forgive you."

He sniffled and wiped his eyes, then reached for her hand again.

"Jack, if that were the only act of violence you'd ever committed, I think I could move past it. But your history haunts me.

When we first got together and you told me about the violence your job required, how you tortured and killed people, it seemed like you had wrestled with those things, that it wasn't easy for you, that you only did what you thought was absolutely necessary. I completely accepted that. When I looked into your eyes then, I felt like I saw into your soul and I trusted you entirely. That's why I've always felt so safe with you. You told me you hoped I'd never think of those things again, that I'd never picture you that way." She rubbed his fingers. "And I haven't, not once in all these years. But I am now. I can't stop picturing you that way now. We always say the only way out is through. Sometimes you have to go back to the beginning to make it through to the other side, to find your way to the ending. I need you to tell me about every person you hurt. I know you were asked to do countless things off the books, so I'm sure it's a long and gruesome list. I can handle it."

His face looked pained. "Tess," he said quietly. "I told you about all of that when we first met."

"No, you told me a list of acts you'd committed. You didn't tell me anything about the situations or the people, the human beings you did those things to. I need to know that you're not a man who takes any pleasure in hurting people. I need to be certain you will never hurt anyone again, because if you did, I would be a part of it. It would feel like it was my fault, like I was complicit. I need to know if how I saw you the night we met was right, if how I've always seen you is right. I need to understand whether or not I know who you are."

He looked down, his breathing labored.

"Jack, I have years of memories with the men who abused me: holidays, vacations, excursions to the park, all kinds of things. I thought those men were good men. I thought they were my family and that they loved me. That belief allowed them to make me feel complicit in unspeakable violence. As an adult, I've always relied on my instincts about people, tried to separate darkness from light. But I'm having trouble trusting myself right now. Seeing Lenny again messed with my head. I need your help. I need you to tell me everything."

He looked into her eyes. "You already have such horrible images of brutality in your mind. I don't want to give you more."

"You're not giving me more. I hope you'll be taking them away. I'm not scared of the past; I'm terrified about what you might do in the future. This is what I need to feel safe with you."

"When you said you had to make yourself numb to survive your childhood, I understood because I had to do the same thing. To do my job, to do the unimaginable things asked of me behind closed doors, required turning everything off. You did it to protect yourself and I did it to protect strangers. I didn't allow myself to feel anything or have anyone in my life, not until Gracie, and then you. You're an angel. Your light saved me. The way you look at me means everything to me, makes me feel redeemed. I don't want to say anything to change that."

She leaned forward, pressed her cheek to his, and touched his head. She pulled back and looked into his eyes.

He caressed the side of her face. "I love you so much, Tess. Now I feel like I'm going to lose you because of things I've done, things I've struggled with, things I truly believed were necessary to protect innocent people and the country I love, but that I'm horrified I had the ability to do."

She took his hand and gently traced the shapes of his fingers, pausing to rub his wedding band. "Jack, do you trust me?"

"Yes, completely."

"Then please tell me everything, and don't leave anything out."

He began telling her about everyone he had interrogated, tortured, or killed in the line of duty. An hour into his recounting, he said, "After the beating, I tied him to a chair. He still wouldn't talk and we were running out of time. I smashed one of his fingers with a ball-peen hammer. Then I told him I was done wasting time, and I pulled out a knife and threatened to start cutting off his fingers one by one. He broke and told us what we needed to know, which led us to someone higher in the cell. He had dark brown eyes. He was about twenty."

Tess dropped Jack's hand. "Enough. That's enough," she whispered.

He inhaled deeply, waited a moment, and stood up. "I'm so sorry, Tess," he said softly, turning to walk away, his head hung in shame and sorrow.

Tess rose and grabbed his hand. He turned to face her. "I'm so sorry, Jack. Please forgive me."

"What?"

"I'm so sorry I had to ask you to do that. Jack, I looked into your eyes and listened to your voice while you were speaking. I know you took no pleasure in anything you did. I can see how tortured you are by it." She paused and put her hand on his cheek. "I see you, Jack. I see exactly who you are, just like I did the night we met and every moment since then. I see you and I trust you with every fiber of my soul."

Tears poured from his eyes. "Oh, Tess, I love you so much," he said, taking her face in his hands and kissing her passionately.

"I love you too, more than anything. You're everything to me, Jack," she whispered.

He picked her up and she threw her legs around his waist. He carried her to the bedroom, kissing heatedly the whole way. He put her down, looked at her, and they started kissing again. After a few moments, he pulled away. "If it's too soon, if you're not ready, that's okay."

"I see only you. Be with me, Jack."

They started pulling each other's clothes off. Jack picked Tess up and laid her across the bed. He started at her feet, kissing her, working his way up to her neck. "You are so beautiful, inside and out. I've missed you. I love you so much," he whispered, running his fingers through her hair. Soon, they were making love, screaming in ecstasy. After, they lay on their sides facing each other, touching each other's faces.

"Are you okay?" he asked.

"Yes, baby. I'm perfect."

"I love you so much, with my whole heart, forever."

"I love you too, more than anything."

They kissed tenderly.

"Oh God, Tess, that was the most beautiful thing I've ever felt."

"For me too."

"I know you were worried we might lose something, but it only gets better between us. Sharing has only made us closer."

She smiled.

"Are we us again? Or at least on our way?" he asked.

"Yes, baby, but I need you to promise me something."

"Anything."

"I know our pasts will always be there, and we will have to learn to live with that darkness, but I don't want any more violence, of any kind, no matter the reason. Only light."

"I promise you, sweetheart."

"Jack, you need to forgive yourself, for everything. It's the only way. You're a good man living in a complicated world and you've always done your best. Forgive yourself."

He brushed the side of her face and nodded. "Tess, you have nothing to be forgiven for, but if there's any part of you that doesn't know that, please let it go."

She kissed him. "I'm trying," she whispered.

"Now I need you to promise me something," he said.

"Anything."

"Please don't ever leave me again. Be my wife always."

She pressed her mouth to his. "Always. And I want you to be my husband forever."

"Knowing everything we've been through, I'd marry you all over again. Marry me, Tess. Marry me again."

She smiled and stroked his hair. "We're already married, baby."

"Let's renew our vows. I know that things aren't magically perfect and we still need time to heal and time together. But when you're ready, let's renew our vows. Will you marry me again?"

"Yes, Jack Miller, I'll marry you," she said, tears in her eyes. She leaned forward and kissed him, lingering to be close to him. "This time we can have your family here."

"We can have anything you want. Tess, I'm so sorry for what I did and for what I put you through. I never wanted to hurt you."

"I know. I'm sorry for what I put you through."

"Promise me one more thing," he said.

"What?"

"That we'll never spend another night apart."

"I promise, my love."

***

After snuggling for ages, Jack said, "Sweetheart, should we make something for dinner?"

"Yeah. I'm famished. Let's cook together."

They turned on some music and made pasta primavera. Jack set the table in the dining room with loads of candles. When they sat down to eat, Tess looked at her plate, frozen. Jack put his hand on hers.

"It's okay, sweetheart. It'll take some time. Just have what you want."

She smiled and started eating. Halfway through their meal, she looked up and said, "Jack, I wanted to talk to you about something. It affects you, and I don't want you to feel pressured because of everything we've been going through."

"Talk to me. What is it?"

"It's about the entertainment offer for *Morning Sun*. I want to do it, but not like with the other ones. In the past, I've just sold the rights and washed my hands of it. I've never even seen any of the movies or shows."

"I know. Everyone thinks it's hysterical, but I've always understood. Omar does, too. You need the characters to live in your mind as you created them."

"Exactly, but with this one, it's different. It's important to me that it's done a certain way. I don't want them to water it down to make it more palatable."

"Good for you."

"I don't want to sell the rights unless they'll make me an executive producer and co-creator."

He put his hand on hers. "I think that's great."

"Getting involved to that degree would impact our lives. We'd have to live in LA for a while. We could stay at our house and the studio could send a car service for me each day, or we could stay in one of the apartments they own. But I'd need to be in LA and would probably work a pretty hectic schedule for at least a few months. It's a lot to ask, and if…"

"Tess, I'm in. I'm completely in. I've told you before that I don't care where we live, only that we're together. I can do my consulting and volunteer work from anywhere. If you get time off, we can take the jet to Maui to unwind. I love the smell of saltwater in your hair."

She visibly relaxed, as if the spring inside her was slowly relieved of its tension. She touched her forehead to his and closed her eyes. She kissed him and then sat back.

"Who knows, they may pass once they hear my terms, or we could have an initial meeting and realize that we have competing visions that can't be aligned."

"I doubt it. I have a good feeling about it."

She shrugged.

"What made you decide to do this?"

"Reading it helped me, even though I wrote it. After all these years, my own words helped me save myself, and us. I know what that book has meant to so many others, and now I understand why. If we take this deal, even more people will be affected by the story. Maybe it will spread some light and help people find their way out of the darkness. Maybe it will help people learn to love and forgive themselves."

"I have no doubt it will."

"Thank you for never making me choose."

He looked at her quizzically.

"Between you and the things and people I love. Thank you for letting me simply be."

"I wouldn't want it any other way."

They continued eating. Tess cleared her plate. They cleaned up, got ready for bed, and made love, their eyes locked. Tess slept peacefully through the night.

The next day, Tess asked Omar to contact the studio and arrange an initial video meeting. They were immediately interested in Tess's proposal. After several conversations over the following days, they agreed to her terms, including leaving the ending unchanged. She then renegotiated her thirty-two foreign translation contracts for *Morning Sun*, tripling the non-recoupable licensing fees just under the wire. She promptly donated the additional earnings to several charities in the US and abroad that help survivors of sexual assault and domestic violence. Per her wishes, the contributions were made anonymously, and her publishing team was directed to remain silent. She also signed a three-year deal with the retail chain, partnering with a charity to donate filled school bags to kids in need. Wanting to be as involved as possible and at Jack's suggestion, she even agreed to personally deliver the bags to several schools and talk to the students about reading, writing, and the pursuit of dreams.

Over the next three weeks, Tess's nightmares decreased from every couple of days to a couple of times a week. Soon, a week had passed with no bad dreams. Her disordered eating slowly improved. She was no longer measuring or counting her food, but simply eating what she felt like, when she wanted. Jack did everything he could to make sure she felt the constant presence of his love. Knowing how painful it had been for him to relive the violence he longed to forget from his days as an agent, she was sure to be extra gentle with her words and touch. Sometimes they would be walking past each other and would stop to touch fingers and look in each other's eyes, their way of saying "I see you." On the third Friday night, they were ready to invite others back into their lives and made a plan to meet their friends at Shelby's Bar.

CHAPTER 15

"I'm telling you, it was so funny I actually choked on my drink," Bobby said. "Like it came flying out of my nose."

They all laughed.

"It wasn't *that* funny," Gina protested.

"Yes it was, babe," he said, pecking her cheek.

She rolled her eyes playfully.

Tess turned to Jack and smiled. He caressed her arm and she leaned back onto him, his arms around her.

"Well, I'll forgive you for telling embarrassing tales because you're doing the sweetest thing ever for me," Gina said.

"Do *not* tell them," Bobby said. "I can't take the embarrassment."

"But it's so romantic."

"Fine," he said, grabbing a handful of pretzels and slinking down in his seat.

"Well, you all know how I love to dance, but this one never dances with me," she said, patting Bobby's arm.

They all nodded.

"He's been taking dance classes! Can you believe it? Isn't that the cutest thing ever?" she said, beaming.

Bobby's cheeks reddened, and he looked down and shook his head.

"Oh come on, it's so sweet," she said, rubbing his arm.

"I think that's great," Tess said.

"Me too," Luciana said.

"Of course you do," Bobby said. "It's all your fault."

They giggled.

Jack raised his beer bottle. "To doing things for the ones we love."

"I'll drink to that," Tess said, craning her neck to kiss him.

They all raised their glasses. "Cheers!"

"So, while Jack and I have been hibernating, we've missed out on hearing about you guys. What's going on with everyone else?" Tess asked.

"Luciana and I have big news. We're moving in together," Joe announced.

"That's wonderful!" Tess exclaimed.

"I'm so happy for you both," Jack said.

"Congratulations," Omar and Clay said.

"We found a place that's just right for us. There's a room I can use as a studio. It has wonderful light, and it's at the opposite end of the apartment from the master bedroom, so when I'm up all night working, I won't disturb Joe," Luciana said.

Tess smiled. "It sounds perfect. I can't wait to find the perfect housewarming gift."

Jack held up his beer bottle. "Cheers, my friend," he said, clinking Joe's drink.

"Well, since everyone's sharing news, I guess Clay and I have our own," Omar said.

Everyone looked at them, wide eyed.

"Butterfly, since you were so absurdly generous with those two-million-dollar bonuses, Clay and I thought about how to best put the money to use. In the spirit in which you live, we've donated half to charity."

"That's so lovely," Tess said, extending her arm across the table and squeezing Omar's hand and then Clay's.

Omar smiled. "We've given half to an organization that addresses hate crimes, and half to an organization that supports survivors of sexual assault."

Tess became misty.

"Now there'll be none of that, Butterfly. You don't want to cause a scene," Omar joked. "Besides, we've been splendidly selfish with the rest of it."

"Well good," Tess said, sniffling. "Then you won't bring the table down."

"Brace yourself, Butterfly. We bought a bungalow in LA. It's about fifteen minutes from your place. We know you and Jack will be spending more time there, plus of course it's closer to your fabulous Maui retreat and I do intend to wear out my welcome in your guest quarters. Clay and I could use our own little tropical sexcapades, after all."

Tess's eyes flooded with hot tears. She and Omar leapt up and threw their arms around one another, holding each other tightly. When they eventually parted, Omar said, "See, now you've gone and caused a scene after all. And you've ruined your mascara, to boot. That's no way for a cover girl to behave."

She laughed and sat back down, nuzzling into Jack. "Clay, how are you able to manage this?" she asked.

"I arranged a part-time gig at a hospital in LA. The two hospitals are affiliated, so it worked out easily."

"We're thrilled," Jack said. "It will be great to see you both more."

"Seems there's a lot of good news at this table. Plus, it will probably be our last time at Shelby's as a group for a while. Should we get another round to celebrate?" Joe asked.

"Actually, before we do that, Tess and I have some news too," Jack said. He rubbed her arm. "Sweetheart, do you want to tell them?"

"Jack and I are renewing our wedding vows. Of course, we want you all to be there."

"Congratulations, guys," Bobby said.

"That's great," Joe added.

"Butterfly, that's wonderful. When's the big day?"

"A week from tomorrow at our place."

"Bloody hell, a writer to the core, always so dramatic. Why the rush?"

"We leave for LA in ten days and we want all of you to be able to come. We're flying Jack's family in for the party. Will you all be there?"

"We wouldn't miss it," Omar said.

They all nodded.

Just then, a slow song came on.

"I have a suggestion," Tess said. "There's a lot of love at this table. Why don't we bring it onto the dance floor before we get that next round?"

They all agreed.

Bobby was the first one out of his seat, his reluctance gone.

Jack reached his hand out to Tess. They wandered onto the dance floor, their hands on one another, staring into each other's eyes.

"You look so happy," he said.

"I am. Every time we leave DC, I feel like I leave a piece of my heart behind because Omar's here. This makes everything so impossibly perfect I can hardly believe it."

He pulled her a little closer to him, their hips swaying together.

She ran her fingers through his hair and continued, "And I'm so happy for our friends. They're all so in love. Speaking of which, what did you say to Bobby?"

"I just gave him a few pointers."

"Seems like it helped. Look how happy Gina is to dance with him."

"Sweetheart, I would look, but I can't take my eyes off of you."

"Jack, I love you so much. You're all that I want forever and always."

"I love you too, baby. I can't wait to marry you again."

CHAPTER 16

Jack was dressed in black pants and a light black cashmere sweater, while Tess sported jeans and a white T-shirt, her hair in a high ponytail as they mingled with their loved ones in the living room before the ceremony. They had their arms around each other as they milled around.

"I can't tell you how happy we are to be here," Mary said.

"Mom, I'm so sorry you guys weren't here the first time we did this. We're so thankful you're all here now," Jack said.

"We are too, son," John said.

"So Tess," Sara said, "you didn't finish telling me about the *Rolling Stone* shoot. I want to hear every detail. Oh, and if I didn't say it already, thank you for sending me the signed copy. I almost died when I saw Mick wrote my name. I can't believe I'll get to meet him at your party in LA."

Tess smiled. "You did thank me and it was my absolute pleasure."

"Yeah, and I want to hear about the *Vogue* pictures," Mikey said. He turned to Jack, "Damn, your wife is smoking." He turned back to Tess and asked, "Did they put something on your skin to make it so, uh… so shiny?"

"Dude, don't go there. Jack will have to kick your ass. I learned that the hard way," Bobby said.

Gina playfully hit his arm and he leaned over and pecked her cheek.

They all laughed.

"Butterfly, do you think it's time to go get ready?" Omar asked.

"Yes, I'm waiting for dessert to be delivered first. Omar, when it's time for cake, will you please make sure to take out the vanilla ice cream and rainbow sprinkles? I want to have my favorite treat today."

"You have a favorite dessert?" Jack asked in disbelief.

"Of course. Everyone does. You love chocolate chip cookies, Omar loves red velvet cupcakes, and I adore vanilla ice cream with rainbow sprinkles."

"How is it possible I never knew this?" Omar asked.

"Well, I don't usually indulge."

Just then, the doorbell rang. "Ah, that must be it," she said, darting off.

"I learn something new about that woman every day," Omar said.

"Ditto," Jack said.

Tess flitted back over, touched Jack's arm, and said, "Honey, would you and Omar mind running down to get the packages?"

He leaned over, kissed her cheek, and said, "Of course not."

The two men headed to the door and returned a moment later with three huge cake boxes, which they placed on the counter.

"Well, that's a first," Omar said, "having dessert delivered by secret service agents."

Everyone turned and looked at Tess for an explanation.

"My friend Kate wasn't able to make it, some pressing national policy meeting or something. She wanted to contribute, so she made our wedding cupcakes."

They all looked at each other, their mouths agape.

"Your life isn't normal," Omar said.

"Dear, are you saying that the president of the United States made us cupcakes?" Mary asked.

"Uh huh. She's a wonderful baker, which is how we became friends, after all. We thought since this was a vow renewal, cupcakes would be more fun than a traditional cake. Anyway, I really should go get changed. Omar, will you help?"

"Your every wish is my command," he replied, taking her hand as they walked off.

As soon as they were out of earshot, everyone erupted in laughter.

"Tess really is one of a kind, Jack," Joe said.

"She sure is."

Ten minutes later, Omar rejoined the group.

"Is she ready?" Jack asked.

He nodded and wiped the corners of his eyes. "Wait until you see her. Your father and I both offered to give her away, but she politely declined, saying, 'I give myself freely to Jack.'"

Jack smiled and told the violinist to play. He took his spot underneath the mantel, where a photo of Gracie sat. He looked out over the faces of their family and closest friends and felt immense gratitude for where life had taken him.

Tess opened the bedroom door wearing a strapless gown—the bodice made entirely of crystals with a full, white, tulle, tea-length skirt—her heart locket, hair cascading in loose, spiral curls. She carried an exquisite bouquet of white hydrangeas. Jack gasped when he saw her. Everyone was beaming as she walked toward him, but her eyes saw only Jack. She handed Omar her bouquet. Jack took Tess's hands and smiled as they waited for the violinist to stop playing. He leaned forward and whispered, "You are breathtaking. I'm the luckiest man in the world." He turned to the group and said, "Since we're already legally married, we decided to do this ourselves without anyone officiating. We just want to tell each other how we feel and share something we've learned since the first time we did this. We thank all of you for being here as our witnesses." He turned to Tess. "Should I go first?"

She nodded.

"Tess, before you, I didn't know if I was capable of letting light into my life, but from the first night we met, you changed me. When we got married, I didn't think I could love you more, but every day since, my heart has grown. You are so beautiful inside and out. You are the kindest, strongest, most inspiring person I have ever known. I spend each day in awe of you. Thank you for making me a better man. You are my lover, my best friend, and my family. When we got married, I promised to love, honor, and protect you for all the days of my life. Now I know what that really means. You've taught me that making someone feel safe and protected isn't about shielding them from external threats, it's about truly *seeing* them, allowing them to breathe, and allowing them to simply be. Sweetheart, I see you and I love you with my whole heart, forever."

Tess's eyes welled. Jack used his fingers to gently wipe her tears.

"Jack, I married you with an open heart, believing that somehow our broken pieces fit together. But it wasn't what was broken that

147

brought us together, it was our complete and total acceptance of each other, as we were then, and as we would become. You are my rock, my joy, and my safety net. I never knew what it was like to have a home, a warm, safe place to just be." She smiled and brushed the side of his face. "When I'm in your arms, I'm home. I never dreamed that it was possible to have this kind of closeness. You've taught me that vulnerability makes us stronger and is ultimately what allows love to flow through us. Because of you, I am more myself and I hope I have more to give you. Jack, you are my everything and you always will be. I see you and I love you with all my heart."

Tears fell from their eyes. Jack whispered, "Together, we are home." He took Tess's face in his hands and they kissed passionately. Everyone burst into applause, and they passed around a tissue box, each guest overcome with emotion.

"Congratulations!" everyone shouted.

"Shall I put your song on?" Omar asked.

"Mrs. Miller, may I have this dance?"

"You most certainly may, Mr. Miller."

A moment later, "All of Me" floated through the air. Jack took her hand in his and put his other on the small of her back. They danced, their bodies pressed closely together, their eyes locked.

"I love you so much," he whispered.

"I love you more than anything," she whispered in return.

When the song ended, Jack said, "I think there's someone waiting for the next dance."

"You danced with the love of your life. Does your soul mate get a turn? May I, Butterfly?" Omar said, extending his hand.

She smiled brightly. "Of course."

Omar turned to the group and said, "Normally Tess and I do this privately, but if she's willing, we have a special song of our own."

"In front of everyone?" Tess asked.

"If you'll have me," Omar replied.

"Always."

Jack played the *Moulin Rouge* version of "Your Song." They started dancing across the room, the full routine from the film. At one point, Omar jumped onto a chair and opened an umbrella he had stashed away. Tess laughed, and so did everyone in the audience. At the end, Omar twirled Tess out and back to him, spun her up in his arms, and then the grand dip. When she stood upright, they were both smiling and giggling. Everyone cheered.

"Well, since I do wear many hats, if it's okay with the bride and groom, I'd like to make a toast now that my dancing obligations are done," Omar said.

"Please do," Jack replied.

Clay passed around flutes of champagne. He handed Tess a glass with sparkling water, and she said, "Actually, today I'll have champagne if you've got an extra one of those."

Jack kissed her cheek and squeezed her hand.

"With pleasure," Clay said, handing her a champagne glass instead.

Omar began his speech. "When I looked around as you were saying your vows, I noticed there wasn't a dry eye in the room. It's because what you two share is so special that we all feel joy just being around you, like we're basking in the glow of the light your love emits. As you two have changed each other, you have also changed us. Thank you for allowing us to be a part of your extraordinary love story. Please, everyone raise your glasses. To Tess and Jack, who have taught us all something about love."

"To Tess and Jack!" they all exclaimed.

Jack and Tess sipped their champagne, making eyes at each other.

Tess then turned to Omar and said, "That was beautiful. Thank you."

"Yes, thank you for everything," Jack said.

"My pleasure. Butterfly, I've only ever wanted you to be happy so that you could truly enjoy this magnificent, wild, utterly surreal life you've created. I'm overjoyed that you and Jack found each other and have found a way to write a new chapter in your love story."

They all smiled.

"Well, I say we open up the buffet and bust into those cupcakes. She's a master at foreign policy, but let's see how well the president bakes," Omar joked.

"Yes, everyone, please help yourselves to some food," Tess announced. "Omar, make sure you save me a cupcake." He smiled. She intertwined her arm with Jack's and pulled him over to a quiet corner. "I want a minute alone with my husband."

He smiled and kissed her. "Did I tell you how beautiful you are?"

She blushed. "Jack, there's something I want, if it's okay with you."

"Whatever it is, the answer is yes."

"Sara and Mikey were telling me about the dog you had growing up."

He laughed. "You want a dog?"

"I've never had one before."

He brushed the side of her face and said, "What kind of dog should we get?"

"Let's go to a shelter. Maybe we can find one that's had a hard time and hasn't had a good family before, one that's just waiting to give and receive love but who needs a little encouragement. We'll know when we see its eyes."

He kissed her lightly.

They stood, staring at each other. She ran her fingers along his temple. He smiled, stroked her cheek, and kissed her softly again. "Sweetheart, you look so happy. What are you feeling?"

"Love. Only love."

EPILOGUE

The Golden Globe Awards

"You're the most beautiful woman here," Jack whispered, his arm slung around Tess. "I saw your ex staring at you."

She smiled. "He's hardly an ex. It was a silly weekend on a yacht, eons ago. You're the most spectacular man I've ever known and the only man for me, and you always will be," she said, lightly pressing her lips to his.

"It's been a big night. Let's make our appearance at the after-party brief. I can't wait to have you all to myself."

"Me too, baby. Ooh, our category is next. You know if we win, they all want me to make the speech."

"Sweetheart, the actors took home every prize. You're going to win, so get ready."

The presenters took to the stage to announce the nominees for Best Drama Series. Moments later, they ripped the envelope open and gleefully said, "*Morning Sun.*" The room erupted in thunderous applause as everyone leapt to their feet for a standing ovation. Tess turned to Jack. He was beaming. He kissed her softly and whispered, "I love you. Congratulations, Mrs. Miller. Knock 'em dead." She caressed the side of his face and rose with the others at her table. Jack watched as she glided onto the stage, her black and white satin gown shimmering, a beautiful balance of darkness and light. Her heart locket was back where it belonged, dangling from her neck. The presenter handed Tess the award and she stood in front of the microphone, waiting for the audience to take their seats. She looked straight at Jack and then turned to the camera in front of her.

"We would like to thank the Hollywood Foreign Press for this great honor, our loved ones for their support, and everyone who worked on *Morning Sun*. We accept this honor on behalf of assault, abuse, and trauma survivors. Please know, we see you. It isn't your fault. No matter what you think, it isn't your fault. Healing is possible. A few months ago, I watched a documentary on PBS about space.

When a supernova occurs, there is an explosion so great that it leaves a black hole, but the shock wave can create the formation of new stars. So too in our human existence there is always the possibility for light. If you can learn to love yourself, that love will become a bridge that will carry you out of the darkness and into the light. And to those who walk with you on that journey, we salute you. To everyone listening, we send you a message of love and light. Thank you from the bottom of our hearts."

SUGGESTED CLASSROOM OR BOOK CLUB USE

1. What do you think about Tess and Jack's relationship? What is special about their relationship, and why is their bond so strong? What role does past trauma play in their love story and how they choose to treat one another?

2. *Supernova* explores the importance of trust in close relationships. How do Tess and Jack navigate this issue?

3. How do Tess and Omar navigate the issue of trust?

4. How do the characters communicate with each other? Consider the verbal and physical aspects of their communication. What do their patterns of interaction reveal about their relationships?

5. *Supernova* suggests that love, in its many forms, can help us heal. Explore this theme in relation to any of the main or supporting characters. What does unconditional love look like in this book?

6. The issue of coping with sexual abuse and trauma is central to the story. What do we learn from Tess's experience? What can we learn from the ways her loved ones both harm and help her?

7. How is masculinity represented in this book? What are examples of both toxic and positive expressions of masculinity?

8. Building on the last question, confronted with the man who repeatedly raped Tess, Jack initially falls into dark patterns of masculinity. What does he learn through this process? How does Tess help him?

9. There is a continuing theme of darkness and light. What is the significance of this theme? What are examples of different ways it surfaces (e.g., black and white photos)?

10. *Supernova* is a book about love, forgiveness, and redemption. What is the overall message about love? Find some examples that support your position.

CREATIVE WRITING ACTIVITIES

1. Bobby, Joe, Gina, Luciana, and Clay are supporting characters. Select one of these characters and write their story.
2. Select one of the characters and look ahead five years. Write a short story based on where you think they end up.
3. If *Supernova* were a play instead of a novel, it would likely include monologues by the main characters. Select a character and write their pivotal monologue.
4. Tess reads from her novel, *Morning Sun*. Use this scene or imagine a different part of the novel to write an original short story.
5. Write an alternative ending to *Supernova*.

QUALITATIVE RESEARCH ACTIVITIES

1. Select several scenes and perform discourse or conversation analysis on the dialogue. For example, use one of the conversations at Shelby's Bar, a conversation between Tess and Jack, a conversation between Tess and Omar, a conversation at the gala, or any other exchange.
2. Research sexual assault and locate peer-reviewed articles or scholarly essays on related issues (e.g., rape culture, family abuse, gender and violence, trauma). Use your findings to write a paper, using Tess's experiences to illustrate or challenge your research.

ART ACTIVITIES

1. Create a visual or audiovisual representation of the scene that Tess recites from her novel, *Morning Sun*.
2. Respond artistically to *Supernova*. Using any medium—literary, visual, or performative—create an artistic response to a theme in the novel or express how the novel made you feel.

AUTHOR Q&A

How would you describe Supernova?

It's a love story that explores trust, violence, forgiveness, and healing in our lives and relationships. It asks the questions: How can we walk through our past traumas? How can we learn to balance darkness and light in our lives? How can love—from lovers, friends, or the art we experience—heal us and help us learn to forgive ourselves and others?

This is the fourth Tess Lee and Jack Miller novel. What inspired you to keep writing about them?

I absolutely love these characters, not only Tess and Jack, but all of their friends. Of all my books, these characters are nearest and dearest to me. I wanted to use these characters to explore love and ultimately write a grand love letter to love itself. Each book in the series explores love at the intersection of another topic. *Shooting Stars* looks at love and healing, *Twinkle* looks at love and doubt, and *Constellations* looks at love and family/intimacy. *Supernova* looks at love and trust. These are universal aspects of our lives and meaningful relationships, so I'm using these characters to explore these fundamental parts of our very human stories. The characters learn lessons along the way that strengthen their bonds and their own identities. I hope the same is true for readers. If *Supernova* is your introduction to these characters, see how Tess and Jack met, in the first chapter of *Shooting Stars*, reprinted at the end of this book.

In Supernova, *the characters experience conflict with one another in ways we haven't seen in earlier novels in the serial.*

In each novel, the characters experience growth and learning and their relationships further develop. In *Supernova*, even the closest bonds are challenged, between both Tess and Jack and Tess and Omar.

Relationships are tested. Life is full of challenges and even those we love most don't always react to things as we might hope, so despite the extreme nature of the examples in this book, the overall story is something I think many of us can relate to. I don't think it's possible to explore love in an honest way without also examining disappointment and redemption.

The characters become more complex in this novel. How did the individual journeys of self-discovery shape your writing?

By exploring challenges that place the characters at odds, there's an opportunity to go deeper into who these people are. They're good people, but like all of us, they aren't always likeable. My intention has always been to answer lingering questions and delve deeper into some of the subjects raised in earlier novels. This is the benefit of a serial; you can build layers of meaning, explore the characters in stages, and fill in their backstories as you go. In *Supernova*, as Tess and Jack struggle to rebuild their relationship, we go back to the beginning of their love story. Things mentioned in earlier novels, beginning with *Shooting Stars*, are addressed in full. For example, Tess's eating issues receive greater focus. While our heroine evolves in each book, for me, it's in *Supernova* that Tess really comes into her own. With this newfound strength of self, I'm excited to share what's next for her.

Does this mean you'll write more books about Tess and Jack?

Yes. There's one more novel: *North Star*. At the end of *Supernova*, Tess and Jack learn to balance darkness and light. I'm excited to show you what they learn next and how they decide to move forward in their lives. I can't rule out writing more about these characters because I love them so much. For now, *North Star* is the planned conclusion. I love where they end up and the growth we see. The last lines bring me to happy tears.

What do you hope readers will take away from this book?

To be gentle with ourselves and those we love. It may be a cliché, but it's true that in order to love others, we have to learn to love ourselves. To do so, we have to forgive ourselves and let go of shame and regret. This is hard. These feelings run deep, and sometimes we don't even recognize them. Redemption is possible. We can be the heroes of our stories.

SHOOTING STARS, CHAPTER 1

"How's your son doing in school?" Tess asked the bartender.

"Really well. He especially loves the history course he's taking."

A man came in and sat two stools down from Tess. They looked at each other and smiled in acknowledgment.

"Hey, Jack. The usual?" the bartender asked.

Jack nodded. "Please."

Tess continued chatting with the bartender as he served Jack a bottle of beer. "The humanities are so important. It's a shame they're undervalued," she said.

"You're the expert," the bartender replied.

Just then, a different man sidled up to Tess. "You have the most beautiful brown eyes," he said.

"Do I?" she asked.

"And the way your hair flows all the way down your back. You know what they say about dirty blondes?"

"I don't think you should finish that sentence," Tess said.

"I've been watching you. Can I buy you a drink?" he asked.

"No, thank you," she replied.

"Come on, just one drink. I'm a nice guy."

"No, thank you," she said, turning away.

The "nice guy" opened his mouth to protest, but Jack stood up with an imposing air and said, "The lady said no."

The man huffed and walked away.

"Thank you," Tess said.

"Don't mention it. I did feel a little sorry for him, though. You are beautiful and I can't blame him for taking a shot."

Tess smiled and pulled out the stool next to her. "Please, scooch over. Let me buy your drink."

He smiled and took the seat next to her. "My name is Tess Lee," she said.

"Jack Miller," he replied. "But it's on me. Yours looks nearly empty. What are you having?"

"Sparkling water. I don't drink. It's just a personal choice," she replied.

"Another sparkling water for my new friend," Jack said to the bartender. "So, Tess, what brings you here by yourself?"

"I was supposed to meet my best friend, Omar, but he had a last-minute emergency. His partner, Clay, was pulled over tonight and it became an incident."

"What was he pulled over for?" Jack asked.

"Being Black," Tess replied. "Clay is a surgeon and was on his way home from the hospital. He was pulled over for no reason and harassed. It's happened to him before. Once, he was on his way to an emergency at the hospital, and he was detained even after he showed his hospital ID. It's egregious. Anyway, I told Omar to stay home with him. They need time together to process and decompress. I was already in a cab on my way here, so I decided to come anyway. I moved to DC from LA about six months ago and I don't have that much of a life yet, I suppose. And you?"

"My friends ditched me. We usually get together on Friday nights at a different bar, but they all had to stay late at work. This place is right down the block from my apartment."

"So, what do you do?" she asked.

"I'm a federal agent with the Bureau, working in counterterrorism. I joined the military right out of high school, Special Forces. I was in the field, often deep undercover, until about a year ago, when I took a desk job as the head of my division."

"Wow, you're like the real-life Jack Bauer. You even look a little like him, with that whole rugged, handsome, hero thing you have going on," she said.

He blushed. "I promise you I'm no Jack Bauer, even on my best day. People thought that character was so tragic, but the real tragedy is that Jack Bauer doesn't exist and you're stuck with guys like me."

She smiled. "What made you choose that line of work?"

"My father was in the military and then became a firefighter. The idea of service always seemed important. I wanted to serve my country, to protect people. It's hard to explain, but when I see someone innocent being threatened, I'm willing to do whatever is necessary to protect them. I know it sounds cliché, but I feel like it's my purpose in life."

"That's noble," she said.

He shook his head. "The lived reality often isn't. When you spend most of your life in the abyss, it gets pretty dark."

"A residue remains, right?" she asked.

He looked at her intently, a little surprised. "Yes, exactly."

"I understand. You convince yourself it's all been for something that matters more than you do, that whatever part of yourself you sacrificed was worth it, because it simply has to be."

He looked at her as if she had read his innermost thoughts. "Yes," he said softly. "Tell me, what do you do?"

"I'm a novelist."

"What are your books about?" he asked.

"That's a hard question to answer. I guess I wanted to write about everything: what it means to live a life, why it's so hard, and how it could be easier. Perhaps my goals were too lofty, and in that respect, each book fails more spectacularly than the one before."

The bartender smirked.

Tess wistfully said, "Maybe reality can never live up to our dreams."

They continued talking, completely engrossed with one another. Two hours later, Jack said, "I live nearby. Do you want to come over for a cup of coffee?"

Tess looked him straight in his warm, blue eyes. "I'd love to."

Jack threw some money down on the bar to cover both tabs. The bartender said, "Ms. Lee, are you sure you're all right? I can call you a cab."

"You're very kind, but I'm fine. Thank you."

Jack opened the door and held it for Tess. "Do you know the bartender?"

"Just met him tonight," she replied.

"Down this way," Jack said, taking her hand as if it were completely natural. They approached a homeless man on the corner asking for money. Tess walked right up to him, pulled a twenty dollar bill from her pocket, and handed it to him. She held his hand as she passed the bill, looked in his eyes, and said, "Be well."

As they walked away, Jack said, "That was really sweet, but you should be more careful."

"I trust my instincts," she replied.

When they arrived at Jack's small apartment, he took her coat. She glanced around and noticed the walls were completely bare. "How long have you lived here?" she asked.

"About nine years," he replied. "Can I get you some coffee or something else to drink?"

She shook her head and meandered over to his bedroom. He followed. He took the back of her head in his hand and started to kiss her, gently and with increasing passion. He pulled off his shirt and they continued kissing. He pulled back to look at her and she noticed the scars on his body: two on his right shoulder, another on his abdomen, and smaller marks along his upper arms. When he noticed her looking, he turned around to lower the light, revealing the gashes across his back. She brushed her fingers along the deep marks. "I'm sorry," he said. "War wounds. A couple of gunshots. Some other stuff from when I was in the Gulf. I know it's gruesome."

"It's wonderful," she whispered.

"What?" he said.

"I'm sorry, I didn't mean it that way. It's just that I've never seen anyone whose outsides match my insides."

He looked at her sympathetically.

"I was abused when I was little. My grandfather and my uncle. It started when I was eight. No one can see my wounds, but they're there."

He stood still, looking at her.

"I'm so sorry. I've never shared that with any man I've been with in my entire life, and I just met you. That has to be the least sexy thing ever. I'll leave," she stammered, trying to walk past him.

He took her hand and pulled her back toward him. He cupped her face in his hands, gently caressed her cheeks, and kissed her. They made love with their eyes locked on to each other. Afterward, he held her in his arms and said, "That was so special. Spend the day with me tomorrow."

162

"Okay," she replied, and they fell asleep, their limbs entangled.

***

The next morning, Tess awoke to find a note on the pillow beside her that read, "Went to get breakfast. There's an extra toothbrush on the bathroom counter. Back soon."

She brushed her teeth, and by the time she was done, Jack had returned.

"Hey, sweetheart," he said, as if they had known each other for years. He pecked her on the cheek. "I didn't know what you like so I got bagels, muffins, and a fruit salad. Do you want coffee?"

"Yes, please."

He poured two mugs of coffee and they sat down at the small table. "What kind of food do you like, anyway?" he asked.

"I'm a vegetarian. I don't believe in hurting living beings."

Jack looked down.

"Innocent beings," she said.

He smiled. "I guess that's why you're so tiny."

She started picking at the fruit salad. Jack noticed that she was moving it around with her fork, almost like she was counting. He looked at her quizzically.

"I'm weird with food. I don't eat that much. It's kind of a control thing," She paused, keeping her eyes on her breakfast. "I have problems."

He reached across the table and put his hand on hers. "That's okay. We all have problems. They make us human."

They spent the day together, talking, watching TV, and walking around his neighborhood. They got Chinese takeout for dinner and made love twice more. Sunday morning, Tess realized she'd missed a dozen calls and text messages from Omar. She called him while Jack was making coffee.

"I promise, I'm fine. I'm sorry I worried you. I met someone. His name is Jack. He's special... Well, if he is holding me hostage, don't pay the ransom. I want to stay... I'll text you all about it... Okay, love you, too. Bye."

"He was worried about you?" Jack asked.

"He's been looking out for me for a long time. We talk every day, but I guess I was too preoccupied yesterday," she said, slipping her hands around his waist.

"Sounds like a good friend," Jack said.

"He's more than that; he's my family. He moved here a year ago and convinced me to leave LA so we could be in the same city. But enough about him. Right now, I'm only interested in you. Come here," she said, walking backward toward his bedroom. Just as he was about to touch her, she grabbed a pillow and walloped him.

"Oh, you're in trouble now," he said, darting for a pillow. They tumbled onto the bed, laughing.

They spent the rest of the day lounging around Jack's apartment, reading the Sunday newspaper, and sharing stories. That night before they went to sleep, Jack said, "I don't want the weekend to end. Do you have to work tomorrow?"

"Well, I do work for myself. Can you take the day off?"

"I once took two weeks off, but other than that, I've never taken a single day off in over twenty years. So yeah, I think I'm due for a personal day."

***

The next day, Tess and Jack went for a walk and ended up at a local park. They sat on a bench, huddled together in the chilly, late autumn weather. Suddenly, a little boy ran over and tugged at Tess's coat sleeve.

"Do you have superpowers?" he asked. "My dad says you do."

"Excuse me?" she said.

His father came running over. "I'm so sorry if he was bothering you, Ms. Lee."

"Not at all," she replied with a gracious smile.

"I'm a librarian. I want to thank you for everything you've done," he said.

"My pleasure," she replied. "Thank you for what *you* do."

The little boy tugged at her sleeve again. "Well? Do you have superpowers?"

His father laughed. Tess looked at the boy and lowered her voice conspiratorially. "I'll tell you a secret. Everyone has superpowers, they just don't know it."

"Even me?" he asked.

"Especially you," she replied.

Jack smiled.

The man took his son's hand. "I think we've bothered these people enough. Thank you again, Ms. Lee," he said, leading his son down the path.

Jack looked at Tess. "That was so sweet, what you said to that boy."

She leaned over and kissed him.

"What was the deal with his father? It seemed like he knew you."

"I did some volunteer work for the library a few months ago," she replied.

A few little girls came skipping past them, drawing their attention.

"It's starting to get cold. You want to go to a movie?" Jack asked.

"Sure."

After the movie, they went to a neighborhood Italian restaurant for dinner. The maître d' greeted Tess like an old friend. "Ms. Lee, such a pleasure. We have our best table for you."

"I guess you've been here before," Jack said as he pulled out her chair.

"Jack, listen to the music," she said.

"Sinatra – the best."

"Let's dance," she said.

He looked around. "I don't think they have dancing here."

"But I love to dance," she said.

He stood up, took her hands, and they danced by the table. "You know, I'm not much of a dancer, but I promise to dance to as many slow songs as you want."

"Maybe someday we'll have a special song," she said, nuzzling into his chest.

Later, when they got back to Jack's apartment, he led her to the couch with a slightly serious look. "I need to tell you something."

"What is it?" she asked.

"You've seen the scars on my body, but there's another side of it. Tess, I've done things – things that may be unimaginable to someone as sweet as you, things I had to do to protect innocent people." He proceeded to tell her every act of violence he had ever committed, his life laid bare at her feet. The list was long, the death count high.

When he finished, she said, "You did what you had to do for your job. I don't understand why you're telling me this."

"Because I'm in love with you. I'm completely madly in love with you and I've never felt that way about anyone. With the things I've done, I don't expect that you could ever feel that way about me, but I needed you to know who I am." He looked down.

She stroked his cheek. "Jack, I'm in love with you, too. I spent our first night together memorizing your face: every line, edge, ridge, pore. I knew you were the best thing that would ever happen to me and I was afraid the memory would have to last a lifetime."

"I feel like the luckiest man in the world."

"Jack, let's not worry about all of the details of our pasts. I want to leave the pain behind and just love each other now."

He smiled. "Okay, but maybe I should at least know how old you are and when your birthday is."

"Thirty-eight, and I never cared for holidays, including birthdays."

"Got it. Forty-two and you're the only present I'll ever need." She smiled.

"Let's go to bed," he said.

The next morning, Jack went to work and Tess went home. At the end of the day, they met at his apartment. "I have something for you," he said, holding out a velvet box. "I was passing an antique store and saw it in the window."

She opened the box to reveal a gold heart locket. She beamed and her eyes filled with tears. "Jack, it's the best present I've ever received," she said, putting it around her neck. "I'll wear it every day."

"You have my heart, Tess. My whole heart, forever."

"Promise me something. Don't ever buy me another present again. Nothing could ever be better than this."

"I'm hoping life is long. That's a lot of birthdays, holidays, Tuesdays," he said.

"Flowers. You can always get me flowers if you want to," she replied.

"Which ones are your favorite?"

"White hydrangeas. I never buy them for myself," she said.

They kissed, and then Jack got up and turned some music on. He reached for her hand. "Let's dance."

The second song that played was "All of Me." Two lines into the song, Jack said, "This is our song, I just know it is. Okay, baby?"

She nodded and rested her head on his chest.

They continued to work each day and spend each night together. Thursday night, Tess made eggplant parmesan, which she brought over to share with Jack. While they were eating, he said, "My friends and I go to this place called Shelby's Bar every Friday night. I told them all about you and they really want to meet you. Will you meet us there?"

"Of course," she said. "Tell me about them."

"Joe is in his mid-fifties. We've worked together for about fifteen years. He's a class act. Bobby is young, twenty-nine, and the nicest, most laid-back guy. He joined the Bureau three years ago, but I feel like I've known him forever. His girlfriend, Gina, is an elementary school art teacher. You'll like her."

"Sounds great. What do you think about bringing an overnight bag and staying the night at my place after we hang out with your friends? It's about time you see it. Omar and Clay are coming over for brunch on Saturday and I'm dying for you to meet each other. Will you?"

"Absolutely," he replied.

"Jack, you know how people always talk about all the things they want to do or see in their lifetime? They don't even mention being happy because I suppose they think that's just a given."

"Yeah."

"Happiness has never been a given for me. I guess I pursued other things," she said.

"Me too," he replied.

"But I'm so happy now, with you."

"I love you so much, Tess."

"I love you, too."

ABOUT THE AUTHOR

Patricia Leavy, Ph.D., is an independent scholar and bestselling author. She was formerly Associate Professor of Sociology, Chair of Sociology & Criminology, and Founding Director of Gender Studies at Stonehill College in Massachusetts. She has published over thirty-five books, earning commercial and critical success in both nonfiction and fiction, and her work has been translated into numerous languages. Her recent titles include *The Oxford Handbook of Methods for Public Scholarship*; *Handbook of Arts-Based Research*; *Research Design: Quantitative, Qualitative, Mixed Methods, Arts-Based, and Community-Based Participatory Research Approaches; Method Meets Art: Arts-Based Research Practice, Third Edition; Fiction as Research Practice; The Oxford Handbook of Qualitative Research, Second Edition*; and the novels *Constellations, Twinkle, Shooting Stars, Spark, Film, Blue, American Circumstance*, and *Low-Fat Love*. Over the course of her career she has also served as series creator and editor for ten book series with Oxford University Press, Brill | Sense, and Guilford Press, and is cofounder and co-editor-in-chief of *Art/Research International: A Transdisciplinary Journal*. A vocal advocate for public scholarship, she has blogged for numerous outlets, and is frequently called on by the US national news media. In addition to receiving numerous honors for her books, including American Fiction Awards, Independent Press Awards, USA Best Book Awards, and a Living Now Book Award, she has received career awards from the New England Sociological Association, the American Creativity Association, the American Educational Research Association, the International Congress of Qualitative Inquiry, and the National Art Education Association. In 2016, Mogul, a global women's empowerment network, named her an "Influencer." In 2018, the National Women's Hall of Fame honored her, and SUNY-New Paltz established the "Patricia Leavy Award for Art and Social Justice." Please visit www.patricialeavy.com for more information or for links to her social media.

Printed in the United States
by Baker & Taylor Publisher Services